BACK IN THE GAME

CHRISTOPHER KEENE

Back In The Game

Future House Publishing

ISBN: 978-1-944452-81-0

Editing by Mandi Diaz
Copyediting by CreelaBelle Howard
Interior design by Hannah Earl

Dedicated to Jack Gifford. Thanks for dealing with the trash.

Chapter 1
A Lucky Find

This is the last time I train in the Penance Peaks by myself!

Cold sleet rained down from the dark clouds. Frank's heavy boot sunk deep into the snow until it hit the frozen rock below. He'd heard that a Heavy climbing the Alps was a sure-fire way to gain quick experience, but at a cost.

All extreme environments in the Dream State gave the player a level of discomfort that was tantamount to masochism. It only made sense—after all, the game designers didn't want everyone who played it to be overpowered in their first week.

Flipping up the visor of his helmet, Frank squinted into the chilly breeze. He could almost see the entrance to the cave that held the Tertiatier Dungeon's Gateway. He'd heard a rumor that a Wanted Ranked player had gone missing from the game after entering it and that his ghost now haunted Rubik's Castle.

Noah-something? Something-Noah? Maybe if he'd been on

the Wanted Boards for longer than a week, I'd have learned his name. Mostly, I just want to know how he managed to get Wanted ranks in Prima and Secotier dungeons so fast. The theater district's weekly rankings never mentioned him again after he vanished...maybe he cheated and got kicked off?

A sudden, howling wind set his teeth chattering. When he started his climb, he thought his tolerance to the cold would rise to the point that the temperature wouldn't bother him, so he hadn't visited other dungeons to steadily increase his temperature tolerance and strength stats. Now he wasn't sure if it was possible to climb the mountains without a mount. He was regretting that he didn't have enough Moola to buy a horse or something that could carry him to the top.

He heard the sound of crunching snow behind him and suddenly remembered another reason why the Penance Peaks were such a great place to train... and die. He turned to see a spotted Mountain Lion prowling on a boulder, baring its fangs and snarling at him.

Fortunate to see it through the snow before it could attack, Frank flicked down his visor, equipped his Broadsword in a flash of light and raised it high. When the Mountain Lion leapt at him, he quickly stepped to the side and smashed the heavy blade into the beast's back. The lion let out a yelp loud enough to draw every monster in the region.

Didn't expect a Heavy to be that fast, huh?

The large cat rolled to a stop on a ledge that led down a steep slope. Deciding to finish off its remaining Hit Points, Frank stalked forward, the weight of his sword dragging down the arm that was already heavy from his full suit of plate-armor. He planted his boot on a jagged ledge of ice and lifted his sword. He was just about to swing it when the ice crumbled, and the overall weight of his armor made him tip to the side.

"No, no, no!" He waved his arms to stop himself from going over, but soon realized his attempt to regain his balance was futile. "Oh, come on!"

He began to roll, making his sword vanish so he didn't cut himself. The fine powder flew as his vision went from sky to snow to sky again before the slope ended against a dark cliff face. His armor stopped him from losing too many Hit Points but he bounced off and landed on his face in the frozen slush. Groaning, he looked up, hoping that no monsters had followed him down. For some reason, a portion of snow ahead of him was glowing a bright green.

What the heck's that?

He rose to his knees, seeing something hidden in the snow that was lighting the cliff face in a green hue. His eyes widened and he scrambled forward on his hands and knees toward it. Hoping for a rare item, his thick gauntlets dug into the snow until the glow shone through the slits of his visor. It was an orb, and as his hand clutched it, the item's information popped into his vision.

— ACQUIRED 'TRANSFER ORB' —

I can't believe it. How…? Why is such a rare item hidden all the way up here?

Frank laughed as he rose to his feet, raising the Transfer Orb high and shaking it at the sky victoriously. Someone with his experience finding such an item was unheard of. Not only were they uncommon and incredibly useful, but expensive as well. They were so valuable that if he sold it, he could use the Moola to buy a mount that could support a Heavy like him, maybe even four. On the other hand, he could train in Tertiatier dungeons with it, knowing he could use it to escape whenever he needed. The possibilities were endless.

Did anyone see?

He quickly peered around before making it vanish into his inventory, wondering if anyone had followed him. If another player saw that he had a Transfer Orb, stronger players would be targeting him as soon as he entered a Tertiatier dungeon in the hope of stealing it from him. Seeing no one around, he trudged through the snow, following the cliff face back to the path heading down.

He didn't feel the cold as much on his way down. His thoughts whirled with what he could do with such an item, whether he should keep the orb and use it to play chicken in the higher tier dungeons, or sell it to get enough Moola to buy whatever he wanted. Both would be of benefit to him, but both also came with risks. If he kept it, he risked having it stolen, but if he tried to sell it, he risked being grifted by a player willing to sell his name to rare item hunters.

There's only one thing I can do that makes sure I get something from this without the risk of being hunted down. I have to put it up on the Anonymous Auction. If I put it at a high enough price I can get a decent haul from it. Until then I'll be able to use it if I ever need a quick getaway.

He grinned now that his plan was set in stone, leaving the Penance Peaks area of the mountains and making his way down to the Galrinth Fields. If he could get to the city before anyone spotted him, he wouldn't have anything to worry abou—

The sound of a group of players arose from the frozen wind and his gaze shot to the bend in the rock they were emerging from. He shook his head and tried to act casual as he descended the frosted track, although he knew a single Heavy up this high in the mountains was suspicious enough. As long as he didn't try to run, he would be fine.

There were four of them, a guy and three girls, one from each of the different Niches. As usual, the male player was the Heavy in massive armor similar to his own. The two smaller females were a Spellcaster in white robes and a Range fighter in black leathers, but the one that stood out the most was the Warrior. Frank could tell she had altered her avatar to decrease her waist size and increase her hips and bust, as well as make her long hair a blood red. Not only this, but her chainmail ended at her thighs to reveal lean legs. The four of them together were quite a sight.

They look like a normal party. Not a group from a hunting guild.

Their eyes scanned over him as they crossed paths, but other than a slight lull in their conversation, there was nothing that made him feel nervous. He sighed in relief as they moved from sight and he jogged behind the bend, breathing like he had a thousand dollars in his wallet and was expecting to be mugged.

Calm down, Frank. No one suspects you. Just get to Galrinth and put the auction up.

It seemed to take forever for him to reach the Galrinth City. He considered using the Transfer Orb to teleport himself there, but he didn't want to risk any players seeing him reappear. Half of the players going up the Penance Mountains had enough strength and accumulated Skill Points to physically drag him to a Tertiatier dungeon. He'd heard that some resorted to such methods to steal rare items.

Although the Galrinth City was plain in comparison to many in the Dream State, the streets were another story. Thousands of colorful avatars of every Niche filled the wide medieval roads as others flew over the thatched rooftops. The smell of forges and spiced foods wafted from the buildings. He passed the bright blue avatar alterations building and stone forges before entering the Synth Square. Beautiful gardens weaved between the branching turquoise-tiled paths leading to the synth stores, spell shops, and the auction house that rose tall against the clear azure sky.

Frank moved into the hall where dozens of players browsed the available auctions. Frank hadn't put anything up to auction before, but he'd been told by his friend Tessa that the system made it easy for newbies. In the center of the murmuring hall was a panel that rose from the wooden floor when he approached. He stood before the terminal, flicking the screen until the catalogue was replaced with the option to make an auction. He selected the option and a form popped up with the entry commands:

— ENTER THE CODE OF THE ITEM YOU WISH TO AUCTION —

Followed by:

— ENTER MOOLA RECLAMATION PASSWORD—

So the form doesn't ask for a name. That's a relief.

Frank accessed his inventory menu and pulled up the Transfer Orb's item details. Every item had a unique code so it could be identified. With so many items in the game, it was unlikely that anyone could connect the item to him. He memorized the code and then inserted it into the panel: E40Y78Z5

After he had entered the last number, the image of the Transfer Orb appeared on the screen. Although he would keep the item on him, he would get a notification whenever a bid was placed on it. Frank then entered the password to claim the Moola offered by the highest bidder, using the same password he had for his email account. He pressed enter and a new screen appeared, asking him what price he wanted to start the auction with.

He grinned, thinking of a ridiculously high number and ending at 70,000 Moola. As soon as he pressed enter again, the auction was confirmed and a notification popped up in his vision.

— AUCTION CREATED —

He smiled. Tessa had been right; it had been incredibly easy. As he stepped back from the terminal, the panel lowered into the floor. The light on the screen passed over the floor and then up the wall like a hologram before showing his item on the wall with its absurdly large price tag.

Satisfied with a job well done, he made his way to the

hall's exit. As he was about to leave, he took one final look around. Frank saw that there was someone already looking at his auction, a blond male archer in beige leather. The expression on his face appeared determined. Although he doubted the player had enough for the asking price, he thought he might have a potential future bid appearing in his notifications very soon.

Chapter 2

A Daring Rescue

The floor never seemed as fascinating as when I was in the rehab center's patient lounge. That and gravity's effect on how long it took my drool to get to the sterile blue carpet. Whatever drugs I had been prescribed by the doctors, it made my mouth dry, my saliva stringy and my head cloudy.

The only thing that seemed to pierce the murk was the constant agony of loss every time I remembered Sue wasn't going to come visit me. The drug also made me forget, so every time I remembered that I would never see her again was just as painful as when the wound was fresh.

The rehab center was, in fact, an asylum owned by the Wona Company, designed to cater to anyone who had suffered symptoms from spending too much time in the Dream State. Its main purpose was to cover the company's backside from lawsuits against anyone suffering from overdose-induced brain damage, muscle atrophy, or in my case, attempted assassination.

My mother had signed me in after I had returned to reality.

She checked in on me now and then, although it was more a formality considering I couldn't focus on a conversation for longer than five minutes. I felt I should have been telling her something important, but couldn't remember what it was long enough to put it into words.

Maybe it's something to do with the drugs they're giving me?

One of the orderlies at the rehabilitation center looked a little like my friend David, minus his dreadlocks and stubble. It was impossible, of course. David could never have held down such a job with his addiction to the Dream Engine. He might very well end up in here with me.

There was something to do with David that I knew I had to tell someone about. I kept fishing my memory for what it was and kept reeling in an empty hook. Even the bait, the thing that had triggered my thoughts was lost along with why I threw out a line in the first place.

Time drifted like a ribbon in a swift wind, but with the drug making me sleep throughout the day, the nights awake seemed to go on forever. This was especially so after I could walk again and yet couldn't leave my room, the door of which was always watched by a night guard.

If my mother's paying for me to be in here, who's paying to make sure I don't leave?

I heard voices outside my door. The night guard was speaking to someone. I focused on the dull murmur to see if I could make out the words.

". . . if you really need to take a crap, just go. I'll hold down the fort until you get back," a familiar voice said.

"What if someone comes to give me a break?" the guard muttered.

"Didn't you say you just had your break and forgot to go?

So just go already!"

"Alright fine!" the door guard sounded more agitated than convinced. "I'll be back soon."

"Don't push too hard. You don't want to end up getting hemorrhoids!"

Now that tone of voice was familiar, but how? The door to my room then opened and the orderly rushed in.

"Come on, Noah. We're getting you out of here."

It was David. How on earth did David get an orderly job, let alone at a rehab clinic for people whose muscles had atrophied from extended periods on the Dream Engine?

Without a word, David pulled me onto my wobbly feet and wrapped a duster around me. After being paralyzed for a month, I had lost a lot of weight and was as light as a feather. David carried me out of my room and down a side corridor to a fire exit. I recalled I had tried to escape by this fire exit before, but it was always locked.

Does David have a key?

As though to answer my question, David pushed some buttons into a phone, and there was the squealing of wheels outside. Blinding headlights filled the safety glass windows of the fire exit before the bull bar of a four-wheel-drive drove up a ramp and crashed into the double doors. They smashed open and alarms went off. When my eyes adjusted to the headlights, I saw another familiar face behind the wheel.

"Hurry up, get in!"

David helped me into the backseat before getting into the passenger's seat, calling, "Shotgun!"

I sat up just in time to see my door guard running down the corridor toward us. With a click, the doors locked and the guard could do nothing but pull on them and bang on the glass. Brock reversed back down the ramp and into the clinic's car park.

"Hey, he's still running!" David called in amusement.

He was right. The door guard was still chasing us down the driveway as we zoomed past the gated entrance.

"Keep going, man. You can make it!" David encouraged.

"Shut up! I'm trying to drive here!" Brock yelled.

His tires screamed as he turned us onto the main road.

"What's going on?" I asked, feeling suddenly faint from all the excitement.

"What's going on?" David asked incredulously. "We just broke you out of the asylum, that's what's going on!"

Making a lot of noise is more like it.

After a half an hour getaway, Brock pulled over and asked David to take the wheel.

"Noah, we've found the Transfer Orb with the videos on it," he said, turning to lean on the corner of his seat.

Transfer Orb? Videos? What are you . . . ? I shook my head as old memories started to emerge from the fog.

"If you know where the . . . whatever is, what's the problem?" I waved at the four-wheel-drive's cramped interior. "Why go to all this trouble if you already have what you need?"

"It's a little more complicated than that." He ground his teeth. "Someone found it before us and put in an auction for a stupidly high price. Even if we combine all our Moola it still wouldn't be enough to afford it. But there's a dungeon in New Calandor that would give us enough Moola if we all did it together. I managed to recover your account so you can do it as well."

"All?" I couldn't process what he was saying. It was too

much to remember all at once.

"I'll show you when we get there."

"Get where?"

David turned back as well with a big grin on his face. "The Dream State, obviously!"

"Eyes on the road, David!" Brock shouted.

"Right," he turned back. "Give me a break, Brock. You had no idea what I had to do to steal this uniform!"

Brock rolled his eyes. "Give me a break. Isn't your roommate an orderly? Speaking of, I have to leave town, so he'll have to stay with you. I admit, you're not as off the grid as I am, but your apartment is under your roommate's name, right?

David nodded.

"It should take them a while to find out where you live if they begin searching for Noah through his friends. Just make sure your parents don't tell them, either. Who knows? Maybe we'll get lucky and they'll think he's bouncing around the country with me."

"You're leaving us? Way to see this thing through, Brock," David replied.

"I have no choice!"

"Oh, come on, guys," I called, putting a drunken arm around both of their seats. "This is the first time we've all been together like this since high school. Teaming up to break me out of an asylum, now that's a reunion!"

Brock grinned back at me. "I like to think of it more as a daring rescue."

It was strange. Ever since I began my rehab a month ago I had felt weak, as though all of my muscles had been worked to the brink of exhaustion. Simply moving my emaciated body was agony, especially while learning to walk again. Yet now, having finally left reality once again, I'd never felt stronger.

As soon as I appeared outside the Galrinth Gateway and saw the familiar medieval cityscape, I knew Brock had been right. I needed to deal with my issues inside the game before I could deal with my issues in the real world.

The evidence to put Wona away was still in the Dream State, and it took some convincing for me to realize that this was all that mattered. Even so, I was still uncertain about his plan. After the subtle threat insinuated in Wona's last message to me, I was hesitant to return to the place where they tried so desperately to put me in a coma.

Brock appeared from the crowd in his beige leathers. "This way, hurry!"

"Yeah, yeah, I'm coming."

We began moving through the city streets toward the Synth Square. All around us the archaic architecture brought back memories of the first time I had arrived here under Data's tutelage. It was all familiar, not just in a warm nostalgic way, but also in a threatening way. Even now, I was worried that dying here might leave me comatose.

"How can you even be sure it's the same Transfer Orb?" I asked as we passed the shop where Data had brought my first sword, a tarnished copper piece of crap.

"Trust me, I'm sure!" Brock called. "I memorized its item code when I encoded the videos on it. I know it's the same item!"

He led me to the Synth Square and I noticed David standing outside a large wooden building beside the spell shop. As always, his Heavy avatar was wearing its bulky shoulder armor.

"Hey! It's still there," he said, as though he had anticipated the question Brock hadn't asked yet. "No one's made a bid for it yet, either. Not surprising considering only a madman would pay that much for a Transfer Orb."

I went to walk in to see it for myself but Brock held me back by my Spellcaster robes. I was lucky Brock managed to recover my account after I was taken out of the game. Thanks to him I was able to keep my equipment, my abilities, and my stats. However, after what he told me we had to do, I knew I would need them.

"Before you go in." Brock sent me a message and it popped up in my vision. "I sent this message to myself before I encoded the videos of the beta player's overdoses onto it. It's the Transfer Orb's item code."

The message said E40Y78Z5, and as he claimed, the message was dated back to before I had my accident. I nodded and he let go of me so I could enter the auction house. The massive hall was filled with different avatars of each Niche. Many of them were gathered around one section of the wall that portrayed a painfully familiar item in what looked like a hologram. A glowing green orb.

That's it!

I assumed most of the players were more intrigued by the extreme price of the item than the item itself. Brock moved through the hall and gestured me to a panel that rose up from a hole in the wooden floorboards. When it came to chest height, it stopped and he flicked his finger across the screen.

"Read 'em and weep," he said, pointing to the screen.

I didn't want to believe him, but what he'd said was true. The code was the same as in Brock's message. The Transfer Orb we needed to convict Wona was right there and yet we couldn't nearly afford it. It was just as Brock had said after he freed me from the asylum. It had happened only two days ago, yet after going cold turkey from the drugs they had been giving me, it felt like it had been over a year.

"So what's this dungeon called?" I asked as we left the hall and headed back to the Gateway in the town square.

David smirked. "Pirate Cove. Sounds like something out of a Disney movie, doesn't it?"

"The point of it is the treasure we can get there. If all six of us can collect the Moola from there, we should have enough altogether to afford the Transfer Orb." Brock waved his hand as we strode swiftly up the stairs toward the Gateway.

I frowned in confusion. "Six of us?"

"Hello-hello, sick boy!" a familiar voice called.

I turned as another familiar female voice shouted. "Over here!"

I grinned as the three girls came into view. Chloe, Keri, and Siena stood by the Gateway, Siena waving with an extended arm.

"Siena and I really had to push them hard to make sure they could get to New Calandor after how badly they screwed up their last Tertiatier dungeon." Brock gestured to the girls in amusement. "And by them, I mean David."

"Hey!"

Chloe put her hands on her hips as she stalked toward us. "It's the truth, Davey. Keri and I barely even need you on dungeons anymore."

Keri clasped her hands behind her. "You have to admit that he makes them a lot easier, though."

"Enough chitchat!" Siena exclaimed, flicking her red ponytail aside. "Noah's back, we're all happy about it. Can we do the dungeon now?"

"Seconded," I said. "We never know when someone with Moola to spare comes and buys that Transfer Orb. We're in and out of this dungeon. Get the Moola, get the orb, and get out."

"Settle down, Noah," Keri said, as though reprimanding me for being impatient. "We'll get there."

I caught David's eyes and he raised his hands in confusion. "Yeah, sure, man. Whatever works, eh?"

Chloe raised an eyebrow at Keri and we moved to the Gateway. Brock grabbed my shoulder and shook his head. The list of settings appeared with the map of the Dream State, and after choosing 'New Calandor', we vanished from the Galrinth town square and appeared in the last city I had been in before leaving the Dream State over a month ago.

I thought back to the pain of the physiotherapy and learning to be mobile again after my paralysis left me, using a frame just so I could walk.

What a terrible month that was.

Chapter 3
Pirate Cove

New Calandor was not a medieval city in any sense, nor was it a dark ages or renaissance-era setting. It was closer to a Victorian or Regency era in its aesthetics and architecture, which was perfect for a dungeon called Pirate Cove. It was the only city with active vehicles, even if those vehicles were nothing more than horse and carriages.

The brick roads were filled with NPCs wearing the fashion that suited the time, including corsets, parasols, colonial-style white wigs and pocket watches hanging from dark waistcoats. Of course, they were mixed with the usual diverse rabble of the player avatars. I followed Brock and Siena through the crowd with Chloe and Keri at my elbows and David trailing behind.

It's like the whole group is back together. That is, except for Data.

"Remember everyone, Pirate Cove is a Tertiatier dungeon. If you get killed there by another player, they can steal whatever you have equipped," Brock said.

Chloe groaned. "I know Noah forgot stuff for a while, but you don't need to state the obvious, Brock."

"Redundancy isn't always a bad thing. It prevents misunderstandings."

To be fair, I sort of appreciated the reminder that just because I wasn't at risk of slipping into a coma, there were still stakes if I was killed here.

Siena rolled her eyes. "You see, kids? Being good at the game isn't all it's cut out to be. You have to be obsessive about this kind of stuff, too."

"It's why he's so good," David said in his defense.

Siena's eyes shifted and she murmured. "I could beat him."

Siena may have had one of the Color Blades, but I wondered if that would matter against a Range Niche like Brock if she couldn't reach him. Then again, I wouldn't put it past Siena to take a few arrows to get to him.

Keri gave me a sympathetic look. "So how was your treatment?"

I smiled. Trust Keri to actually care about my well-being in the real world.

"It was hell, if I'm honest. Relearning to walk after being paralyzed for a month was painful work, but the drugs and professional physios my parents paid for made the process a whole lot shorter. I'm still having trouble staying on my feet for long periods of time though."

"Well, it's good to know you're on the mend then," Keri replied, giving me her angelic smile.

Chloe bumped her hip into mine. "Must be good to get at least the illusion of being able to stand strong again."

I nodded grudgingly. I couldn't deny that the illusion

of having strength was far better than no strength at all. However, the idea that I could return to my weak body without the evidence I needed to put Wona away was something I dreaded most of all.

"How far away is the Gateway from the city?" I asked, seeing that we were approaching the ships anchored in the harbor.

It was then that I saw a pathway leading down the harbor. The area around the docks was filled with the sound of bustling sailors and seagulls calling in the overcast sky. Many large boats filled the water, but we only had a clear path to one. We followed it up a boarding plank onto the ship's deck.

"Who said the Gateway was outside the city?" Siena asked as the Gateway on the ship's deck appeared before us.

David nodded with his bottom lip stuck out. "It makes sense. If we're going to run into pirates, what better way to do it than sailing on a flash ship like this?"

Chloe stepped up to the Gateway. "I highly doubt we'll be setting sail. This Gateway will probably just teleport us straight to the cove."

"Let's find out," I said.

We selected the option to enter Pirate Cove together.

Chloe wasn't entirely wrong. Although the sails lowered and we launched off into the ocean, we didn't see the journey itself. We were simply teleported to a new area. I knew we wouldn't see the journey back either considering the state of the boat we were on after appearing in the new dungeon.

The thing was a mess with a hole smashed through the broken deck, torn sails, snapped masts and splinters of wood spread out along the stern. The bow was gone, seeming to have crashed right into the rock when entering the cove.

It was dark inside and I heard Chloe groan when a cold drip of water fell onto her hair. With the cold and broken wood everywhere, I was almost tempted to say *shiver me timbers,* but thought even that joke was below me.

"Hah, pretty haunting place, isn't it?" Brock said.

"Where're all the pirates?" Siena asked as she pulled out her rare Color Blade, the Ruby Edge lighting everything with its red glow.

Brock put a hand on the side of the boat and jumped from it onto the damp rocks. "Further in, with all the other players doing this dungeon. Watch each other's backs and don't go running off. I'm looking at you, Siena."

Siena placed an offended hand on her large chest. "Would *I* do something like that?"

The fact that she had done this in almost every dungeon I had completed with her made me chuckle. We followed Brock off the boat and began tailing him into the darkness of the cove, Siena's Ruby Edge lighting the way.

The red glow was soon overtaken by lanterns that lit a path of empty bridges over the water going further into the cove. Despite this, Siena didn't withdraw her blade. This was all I needed to see to know that I should be cautious here.

"Be on your guard. These bridges are known points of ambush," Brock warned. "They aren't Chaos Engines, but with the frequency that pirates attack players on them, they might as well be. It's not uncommon for another group of players to take advantage of other parties being attacked either."

"Are the pirates strong?" Keri looked around nervously. "This place gives me the creeps."

"This *is* a Tertiatier dungeon, Keri," Chloe snorted. "Besides, who would be afraid of pirates?"

There was a sudden splash of water and David squealed like a little girl. We all turned to see that a hand had reached out from the water and grabbed him around the ankle. The gaunt face of a pirate emerged, a red bandanna on his head and a sharp knife between his rotting teeth. In shock, David equipped his mace and was about to cave the thing's head in when more hands shot out from the water, trying to snatch at us.

The rest of us jumped back from them, but before we could attack there were clicking sounds all around us, and Brock shouted, "Everyone, hit the deck!"

Everyone but David, who was held upright by the pirate, crouched or fell to the bridge. A volley of projectiles flew in whizzing lines over our heads.

Guns?

Granite sprayed where the bullets hit the opposite wall, many of them pinging off of David's thick armor as he raised his arms defensively.

When the barrage was finished, Brock rose to his feet and raised his hands as two of his own flintlock pistols flashed into his open grip. With puffs of gunpowder, he fired them in the direction of the muzzle flashes and two pirates hit the dirt. The guns vanished from his hands. Like real flintlocks, they could only be fired once.

Where can you even buy *guns?*

Still screaming, David had gone about smashing the heads of the pirates that had emerged from the water, as though angry they had made a fool of him. Siena and I took out another two, me with the familiar Crystal Blades that I had synthed in Lucineer and Siena with her Ruby Edge.

Two more gunshots came from Brock and two more flintlocks vanished from his open hands. I assumed they were the last loaded pistols he owned for he equipped his bow next and began firing arrows.

Chloe finally started tossing her throwing knives at the remaining pirates. As always, her aim was impeccable and she finished them off with ease. What Brock had said about the ambush made sense. If the bullets had hit their targets, we would have been sitting ducks to any passing players that decided to mob us.

The fight was over in a matter of minutes. Keri rose and used a healing spell to recover David's Hit Points, and we all stood, panting.

Siena laughed. "Wooh! Now this is what I call a dungeon!"

"This . . ." Brock gestured to the dead pirates around us before they disappeared, dropping their weapons that we collected. "Is what I call a close call."

Chloe screwed up her nose. "Bah, I hate the smell of gunpowder."

Keri bit her lip and looked down in shame. "I'm sorry . . . I froze a bit."

Chloe patted her back fondly. "It's okay. I did too."

"And weren't you the one ready to chide any of us for being afraid of pirates?" David teased.

"I wasn't afraid!" She snapped back. "It just surprised me is all. At least I didn't scream like a girl!"

"I might have," Keri admitted.

"It surprised all of us." I let the Crystal Blades vanish from my grip. "Let's keep going."

I stalked ahead, crossing the bobbing bridges to the next

rocky edge of the cove, determined to finish the dungeon, but feeling their eyes on my back.

Brock caught up with me, expression questioning. "Having fun yet?"

"I'm here for one reason and one reason alone. On another note, when were pistols allowed in the game?" I asked, grinning from my ignorance.

Brock raised his brow. "You can use different weapons depending on the era you're playing in. As you can imagine in an era of gunpowder like New Calandor, the Range Niche is going to take every advantage of that by using pistols."

How could I have spent an entire month here and not have asked that? I guess I didn't get to another era until the last day. But that does raise the question . . .

"How many eras are there?"

"Only the two for now." Brock shrugged. "But I've heard a rumor that there's a third era dungeon the game designers are creating somewhere in the world."

"More or less modern?"

"It's just a rumor, but I have a hunch that it's something sci-fi." Brock's eyes shot forward as though he had heard something, and he stopped. "Other players . . . up ahead."

I peered into the darkness and could just see the group emerging from the shadows ahead of us. The echoes of their laughter bounced off the cave as their avatars made shadows on the walls.

From their lack of gear, the majority of them looked like they had only been in the game for a few weeks and were pushing their luck in a Tertiatier dungeon. All but one.

I would have recognized that Rhino Leather vest from a mile away.

"This is not good," Brock murmured.

The group of players stopped and stared at us apprehensively.

As our own party caught up with us, the only joyous tone in the group was Siena calling, "Oh, Data! Guiding another set of newbies, eh?"

Chapter 4
Treasure Hunt

Around us the gentle waves rocked the bridge we were standing on. The ruins of shipwrecked boats went further ahead of us from where the second party had come from, but that was far from my notice. The tension in the air between Brock and Data was thick. Besides the fact that Brock had left Wona, there didn't seem to be any real reason for the animosity between them.

"Datalent," Brock said stiffly.

"Brock," Data returned but then smirked. "Or do you still go by Brockodile?"

"Call me what you want and you'd still be wrong."

"And you would still be a coward!"

Siena stepped between them, as though a fight was about break out. "Settle down you two. Besides Data, I don't think you'd want to seem unprofessional in front of your new clients, am I right?"

Data inclined his head and eyed me up and down. "Tsh, you're back in the Dream State faster than I would've imagined, Noah."

"I had unfinished business here."

"Your video evidence against Wona?" His shook his head. "It doesn't exist."

He sounds confident. Wona must have been scouring the Dream State code looking for a Transfer Orb with videos hidden on it.

David raised a hand like he was in class. "We can prove it, it's in the—"

"Shut up, David!" Brock shouted.

Chloe grinned, as though hearing someone else telling David to shut up for a change was amusing to her. It was obvious that Brock didn't want Data to know where the orb was in case he told Wona so they could get rid of it. Brock trusted him about as far as he could throw him.

I stepped forward to stand with Siena. "Listen, Data. I can see you're busy right now, but once we're finished here, we'll be able to get our hands on the orb. If you meet us in New Calandor after we're done, we'll be able to show you ourselves."

Brock raised his hands at me. "Noah, you can't—"

"Brock, I get Data's point of view. He has a code that he stands by and I know that his loyalty is not blind, but conditional." I caught Data's eyes and he nodded in agreement. "He wouldn't work for murderers, not knowingly anyway. So how about it, Data?"

Data shrugged. "I have nothing pressing I have to do after this. I guess I could humor you for a few minutes. I'll meet you at the Chevalier Café in two hours. It shouldn't take you that long to get through this place."

I nodded and our group passed one another as civilly as if there wasn't a single item we wanted from each other. Keri breathed out a sigh of relief as she went around one of the Heavies in the group.

"Wow . . . that was . . ."

"Yeah," Chloe said as she came to my side. "And I thought waiting for pirates to ambush us was tense."

David pointed ahead of us to the boat we were about to cross. "Hey . . . pirate ship."

"Now you're pointing out the obvious, too?" Chloe asked in exasperation.

"Well, we're here for treasure, aren't we? You'd think maybe there'd be some inside their ship."

Brock shook his head. "There's a trick with Pirate Cove. If you don't touch any of the chests until the end and open the final chests in the right order, you get a far greater haul than anything you might get during the dungeon."

"So it's like the Cave of Wonders from Aladdin?" Keri asked. "Touch anything but the lamp and . . . lava?"

"Similar, but not quite." Brock corrected. "More like no Moola."

There was a rough sniggering noise from the hull of the ship. From the massive hole in its side, three pirates emerged wielding jagged sabers. One had an eye patch, one had a peg leg and one even had lace sticking out from his cuffs.

"Mine!" Siena called, running as she swung out her blade.

She cut them down like driftwood and each of them dropped a flintlock pistol or saber after they had vanished. The guns went to Brock, the swords to Siena.

We continued through the cove. More pirate lackeys appeared but were taken out by Chloe, eager not to be outdone by Brock's Range skills again. The bridge crossing the water ended a meter from the rocks and everyone turned to look at me. I grinned as I realized why. It had been a while since I used any of my magic.

I knelt down to the water and rubbed my hand in a clockwise direction while thinking of the water freezing. Instead of a wall of ice appearing in front of us, a bridge of veining ice spread horizontally over the water's surface.

"Thanks!" Siena called and bolted across it.

We followed her, coming through shadows into an open hollow in the cove. What Brock said about being tempted by the other treasure suddenly made sense, and I realized Keri's Cave of Wonders analogy was closer to the mark than Brock gave her credit for. Mounds of gold coins, cups and gemstone-encrusted armor filled the cave.

Although we all stopped to gaze at the bounty of riches, no one looked as keen to rifle through it as Siena. I didn't know if the coins were actual Moola, but if they were, I found it hard to believe that the chest game Brock wanted to play at the end of this dungeon would provide us with more than the mountains of stuff in this room.

Through the hollow was a red throw rug that led to a gold-plated chair, and on it was the dungeon's boss. The pirate sat on the chair like it was a throne. He was wearing a wide-brimmed hat with a large feather and a long red coat with high boots. When my gaze passed over him, a scroll unraveled to reveal the dungeon boss's name was "The Captain." On his hip was a flintlock pistol and a long rapier.

He looks a bit ragged, but who wouldn't be after getting shipwrecked in such a place?

"Get in front of us, David!" Siena called.

"Why me?"

"Because your armor can block the bullets," Chloe said,

rolling her eyes.

"Oh yeah," David moved in front.

As he approached, the Captain drew both weapons, and went into a wide stance, pistol in his right hand, sword in his left.

He called a fierce, "Yar, Matey!"

Instead of firing, he lunged forward, stabbing his rapier into the gap in David's armor, between the plates covering his chest and arm. Using the blade to spin David behind him, the Captain faced us and raised his pistol. On instinct, I raised an Ice Wall in front of us to block the bullets. Brock and Chloe went to either side of the wall and began hitting him with arrows and throwing knives before Siena leapt over the wall, Ruby Edge dancing.

The Captain raised his blade and parried Siena's swift strikes with immaculate fencing skills. My first surprise that the boss could block such blows by a Color Blade was overcome by the fact that he could fire a second volley at us. There was something about his weapon that made him able to fire his pistol more than once.

I keep forgetting that this is a Tertiatier boss!

Keri had finished healing David and used a shield spell to block the bullets as I summoned dual Crystal Blades into my hands. I charged in to assist Siena in the melee. The Captain spun and shattered my blades without so much of a backwards glance before shooting Siena. The bullet caught in her chainmail, but the impact still blew her back and took a chunk of her Hit Points. Fortunately, the boss had forgotten about David.

His mace swung into the Captain's back and he was spun one way by Brock's arrow and the other way by Chloe's throwing knives. He was fighting on the back foot, and like many bosses, this was when the Captain tried something desperate. He leapt to one of the hills of coins and kicked them at us, yelling, "Ya filthy landlubbers!"

"Dodge them!" Brock yelled. "Otherwise this is all pointless!"

Keri used another shield spell to block the coins from hitting David but the Captain then jumped to another pile of loot. He sprayed them at us from all angles and it was only thanks to my speed that I managed to dodge the coins kicked my way.

"There's a space clear of treasure up ahead!" Brock called and we ran toward the chair.

Siena kicked it down to reveal an empty space at the back of the cove. From the five chests spread out around the space, I could see this was the end of the dungeon.

"En guarde, lassie!"

I turned to see the Captain engage with Siena and David once again, and seeing the boss's Hit Points reaching the one-third mark, decided it was time to finish him off.

"Everyone get back!"

They spun to me in confusion, but leapt back from the Captain. I crossed one arm over my chest and flicked it out, spreading Wildfire throughout the cove. It seemed Brock still had some gunpowder left in his inventory, for he threw a bag of it at the Captain. Like a grenade, it exploded as soon as it hit the fire, blowing away the last of the boss's Hit Points. We had won.

"Yo ho . . . yo ho . . . off to Davy Jones' Locker I go," the Captain sang. When the fire dispersed into the air, so did he with an explosion of light.

Having left, a green and red parrot flew in and perched on the tipped over chair, peering at us as we entered the hollow together.

"Is it just me, or are Tertiatier Dungeons getting easier?" Chloe asked.

"We do have Brock and Siena with us," David said as Keri went to work recovering his Hit Points.

As though hearing his name, Brock walked through, calling, "Don't touch those chests!"

"We weren't going to!" Chloe yelled back. "Don't you think pointing out the obvious so much is a bit insulting? Like insinuating we're too dumb to remember something you said from, like, five minutes ago?"

"It's better than risking wasting more time doing this dungeon over again." Brock pointed to the chest furthest away. "But considering you did listen to me, you can do that chest on the end. Noah, David, Keri, you do the other three."

Siena's brow furrowed. "Why do I get left out?"

"Because I know how impatient you get with these kinds of things," Brock exclaimed. "Besides, I saw the way you were looking at those piles of treasure. It must have taken you a great deal of willpower not to pick up some of that pretty armor."

"Oh, whatever!" she scoffed.

We each moved to our different chests and awaited Brock's instructions. We turned to him, his expression focused on remembering what order they were supposed to be opened in.

"When I say your name, quickly open and close your chest, alright?" Brock asked and all four of us nodded.

"Okay. Noah!"

I quickly opened my chest, seeing that there was nothing inside before closing it again.

"Chloe!"

Chloe followed suit, barely lifting the chest's lid before closing it again.

"Keri!"

On the end opposite from Chloe, Keri opened and shut her chest.

"Chloe!"

Chloe's lips pursed at being asked to open hers again, but did as she was told.

Brock opened and shut his own chest before calling, "David!"

David opened his lid right up before slamming it shut. I went next, and then Keri and Chloe again before Brock lifted his own lid and a trumpeted fanfare played over the background.

— ACQUIRED 10,000 MOOLA —

Wow, that's a lot of Moola, but wait . . . was it just me, or did everyone get that much?

My eyes widened in realization. "Did you all just get ten thousand Moola as well?"

"Holy cow!" Keri cried.

"Yeah . . ." David said in amazement. "Hah! That's some secret, Brock!"

"Is that enough to get the Transfer Orb?" Chloe asked.

"With the Moola Noah and I already have . . . it should be."

Brock and I both nodded, while David looked up as though trying to remember what price had been displayed on the auction house wall.

"Convenient much?" Chloe murmured.

"Are we done here?" Siena asked, as though bored already.

"We are, but you might want to go back and pick through what you avoided before." Brock grinned when seeing the surprise on Siena's face.

"You mean . . . I can still . . . ?"

Brock nodded and Siena squealed and rushed off to go wading through the shiny armor. Brock then pulled out a Transfer Orb and gestured for everyone to gather around him. It was just short of the two hours since we had told Data to wait, but that only gave us some time to find the Chevalier Café where he told us to meet him.

"Ready?" Brock asked and we nodded.

With a flash, the five of us passed through the opened Gateway from the dark, damp Pirate Cove into the brick streets of New Calandor.

Chapter 5

Seeing is Believing

Siena met back up with us in New Calandor and it only took us a few minutes to find the place Data had mentioned. The Chevalier Café was a two-storied bar with a high ceiling, glass chandelier and a mezzanine that advertised what looked like a flock of finely dressed peacocks, hosts and escort girls.

We found Data waiting for us at the end of the polished wooden bar looking through his items. At least, I assumed he was by the way he was staring off into space. I moved through the different avatars in the bar toward him.

"Data," I said, Siena waving from behind me to get his attention.

He looked down at us and his jaw tightened.

"You ready?" I asked.

"Tsh, if I'm going out of my way to follow you free of charge, you better have something good to show me."

I inclined my head. "You'll have to come and see for yourself. My friends just sacrificed a crap load of Moola to be able to buy it."

He nodded and got off his stool, murmuring as he passed, "Let's make this quick."

The girls waited for us outside the bar, Brock and David having gone ahead to the auction house to buy the Transfer Orb. With the obvious grudge he held against Brock for leaving Wona after the betas died, we thought it would be better to have them apart until the evidence was in our grasp.

"You were right, it didn't take long for you to return to the Dream State. I was hoping for some peace and quiet before you got back," Chloe said as we made our way through New Calandor to the Synth Square.

We passed shops and other places for players to strategize before doing dungeons together. The area made me feel like I had gone back in time, even more so than Galrinth from how true to the times it looked.

"With how much you talk I could've sworn you liked loud, annoying noises." I returned.

Keri shrugged with a smile. "It explains why she hangs out with me, I guess."

"I didn't mean it that way." I sighed. "I was just talking out of my butt."

"Sounds familiar. I've missed this," Data said sarcastically but then shook his head as though he really had. "How did your treatment go after you got out?"

"Smoothly," I lied. "I can't say the same for the rehab center Wona put me in where they had me drugged up for the last month."

"Tsh, one unprovable claim after another."

We arrived at the Synth Square. Like all Synth Squares, there were multiple pathways going to the many stores in the area. The unique aspect to New Calandor's square was that each path was blocked by tall sandstone walls, like the many-pathed junction of a Gothic maze.

We followed the signs on the walls with arrows pointing to the synth shop where one could synthesize Resource Items into equipment, a weaver's store for using the same items to make garments, the spell and abilities shop where players could buy spells and abilities unlocked in certain dungeons, and the Anonymous Auction Hall.

We moved down the corridor into the hall, looking more like a barn here among the tall buildings than in Galrinth among the thatch-roofed cottages. Avatars were looking at each of the items being auctioned, shining like holograms on the walls. David shoved through the crowd, his face pale.

"Noah, the orb's gone!"

"What?" I felt my heart skip a beat in my panic. "Did someone buy it?"

I should have known it wouldn't be that easy.

"No. Whoever auctioned it just had it removed, which means whoever they are, they still have it."

Data sighed as though this couldn't have been avoided. "Tsh, do you have the item's code? If you do, I could find out where it is."

I nodded, remembering that Brock had a message with the exact code of the item.

Brock suddenly stalked through the crowd from the direction of the panel, having obviously been listening in on us. "We're not giving you the code!"

"Because the item doesn't exist!" Data retorted.

Brock ground his teeth and stepped closer to him. "No, because you'll give the code to Wona and they'll delete it before their secrets come to light!"

"That's bullcrap!"

"Boys, boys!" Siena stepped through, separating them. "There's a really easy way of solving this problem. Data, you give us the software we need to track the item down, and, if you want, you can come with us."

He shook his head. "I'm not allowed to give the software to players."

"Data, this is important," I argued.

"So is keeping my job!"

Something then occurred that I could've sworn I would never hear. Siena began sounding sincere. "Data, you've trusted me with a cracked copy of this software before. I deleted it right after I got what I wanted, just as I said I would. Besides, I think this is a lot more important than finding one of the Color Blades, don't you?"

Data ground his teeth. "Tsh, you were supposed to keep that a secret."

"Data, please." She moved closer to him, her eyes wide while looking up at his ashamed expression. "Whether or not you trust Brock is irrelevant. Trust Noah . . . and trust me."

He nodded. "I'll only give it to you, though. If you're sure about this, if Brock gives you the item's code and I give you a copy of the item tracking software, you'll be able to find the player who has it. But I'll only give you the software if you promise you'll let me see it when you have it."

There was something in Data's voice as he said this, as though he honestly wanted to believe us. Siena nodded and turned to us with her familiar grin.

"Alright then, that settles it! I'll be the tracker and whoever wants to find this thing can follow me."

I nodded. "When do we do this?"

"I'll need a day to get permission to use the software and make a copy for her." Data sighed. "But remember, the item tracking software itself can be tracked by Wona when it's activated. They'll hunt you down if they catch on to what you're doing."

"Being hunted by Wona . . ." Siena walked away, shrugging. "Sounds fun."

Having had the experience of being hunted by Wona, I wasn't sure if I agreed with that sentiment. Nevertheless, once we received the item tracking software, we would be one step closer to finding the Transfer Orb.

Chapter 6
Trust

Frank was well aware he had a lack of conviction with the actions he took in-game. It didn't take much encouragement for him to second guess himself and start to think he was a fool, especially when that encouragement came from Tessa.

They sat in the theater district, facing each other on the stone seats as the teaser trailers for the upcoming expansion played on the screen between two ancient Greek statues. From the videos that repeated over and over, the imagery of blimps, whistles and gears gave off a steampunk vibe.

In a city like Galrinth, the theater looked out of place.

"What were you thinking?" Tessa cried, raising her nimble hands up in exasperation. "Someone would obviously notice the connection between a new rare item being put up to auction and the low-leveled, armored tank who's never entered the hall before! No offence, but you kind of stand out."

"Keep it down, Tess!" *Does she want all of Galrinth to know how I screwed up?* "What did you expect me to do? I had to get rid of it somehow!"

"But not by revealing to everyone that you, one of the weakest Heavies in the Dream State, had it. I'm surprised you haven't been invited to a hundred Tertiatier dungeons already!"

Tessa was right. He had received several invitations to do Tertiatier dungeons.

Despite being small for even a Range Niche, Tessa was one of the few in-game friends that Frank felt he could trust. The elfish blondie had been his friend since pre-school and she had always looked out for him, even during his transition into this new world. Next to his tank avatar, her green-scarfed form looked even smaller simply by contrast.

"Well, you don't put it in a place where everyone can see it!" Tessa slapped her forehead. "I mean, come on! You could have at least altered your avatar before going into the auction house!"

"Okay, okay, look!" He made his menu visible for her to see. "It's no longer up for auction! I've closed it, happy now?"

"Happy . . . ? Yes, I'd say I'm happy you're not gonna get lured and slaughtered for it." Tessa raised her brow, letting a narrow grin spread over her lips. "I'm just trying to make sure you don't get a bum deal with it, Frank, that's all."

"And what do you suggest I do, oh wise one?"

Tessa grinned and raised a finger. "I've got this friend who would be willing to take it off your hands for a good price."

"And who would this friend be?"

"His in-game name is Dice, and he's one of the few Wanted ranks in the Dream State with red hair. I'm just saying this in case you want a way to recognize him when you two meet up. He can be trusted to keep his mouth shut. I won't even tell him your name if you don't want. I'll just give you a time and place that you can arrange to meet and make the trade."

Frank nodded. "How much?"

"Fifty thousand."

I guess that's only twenty thousand less than what I asked for.

Frank nodded. "Alright, that'll do I guess."

"That'll do?" Tessa asked in outrage. "The most Moola a single player can get in one dungeon is ten thousand! You'd be getting five times that much!"

"Okay, okay, fine! I said I would go. When are you going to arrange it for?"

"I'll message him now and see when it suits him."

Frank's brow furrowed. "Wait, if you know how much he's willing to buy it for, you must have told some people about it when shopping around to see if anyone was interested."

Tessa shrugged. "As I said, Dice is trustworthy, and I never mentioned your name. I'll message him and we should do a dungeon. Hopefully he'll get back to us by the time we're done and you can get it sorted by tomorrow or the next day. Just try to stay away from any Tertiatier dungeons until then."

Frank nodded and stood up. "You know I haven't accumulated enough Skill Points to go into a Tertiatier dungeon on my own anyway."

"Sure, but you never know whose invitation you might get in the next few days from Wanted rank players hoping to do you in." Tessa got up and followed him out of the theater district toward the Galrinth Gateway. "Anyway, where do you want to go? Toena? Yarburn? Lucineer? Onjira?"

Frank grinned, stroking his chin. "Hmm, I'm thinking Japanese tonight. What do you think?"

Tessa smiled her pixie smile and nodded. "Yeah, Japanese sounds good!"

The Emperor's Maze was a dungeon on the eastern providence of Toena. It was a rather unique Primatier dungeon. Not only was there a sure-fire method of getting through it by sticking to the right hedge wall, but by using a Heavy of Frank's size, one could bottleneck enemies while a Range teammate like Tessa could take them out.

They made a great two-person team for such a dungeon and it was the third time they had done it in the last two weeks. Having lots of bird enemies that would swoop in from a distance allowed Tessa to increase her Skill Points quickly.

The maze eventually led to the high verandah of the palace, and the climb would increase his speed even further for whatever dungeon he decided to do next. Doing the dungeon together was mutually beneficial.

The vine monsters that rose from the maze hedges were annoying. They whipped around and tried to tangle and trip him, but it was nothing his Broadsword couldn't deal with. When one wrapped around his armored leg, he severed it, jumped another and ran to catch up with Tessa's darting form.

Tessa ran ahead, leaping from hedge to hedge, firing her

mini-crossbow and reloading it as soon as she landed. Her arrow tips were poisoned, so if her first attacks didn't kill the monster, all it took was a simple charge from Frank to finish them off.

Attempting to get himself free of another vine, a massive snake arose from the hedge, its python head rearing up to strike. He screamed in horror and swung at it, but it darted back. Tessa flipped over the pathway and fired an arrow at the back of its head. The impact of the blow drove its head forward enough for Frank to lunge in and chop it off.

Ah! I hate snakes!

He put more effort into the blow than he meant to and fell on his face. Sometimes when he was afraid he did more damage to himself than the dungeon did. The constant encounters here allowed him to build up Skill Points to decrease his already light weight stat in order to move faster. This made him less bogged down than a usual tank as they had to sacrifice speed for the heavy armor they could wear and weapons they could wield.

"Hurry up, Frank!" Tessa called.

He panted as he ran down the last path leading out of the maze, up the steps, and onto the Emperor's Palace verandah. There, the final haul of the dungeon awaited. The palace was covered with gold, twirling ribbons, massive gold bells, and was surrounded by several fishponds. Tessa waited at the top of the stairs, jumping up and down and waving her arms.

When he arrived at the top, he put his hands on his knees and breathed heavily. Tessa patted him on the back and then turned to the items waiting for them. They included several of the Resource Items found in the maze itself as well as a Dragon Dagger. Frank allowed Tessa to take the dagger considering how ridiculous he would've looked wielding such a tiny thing.

"Thanks . . . hang on." Tessa looked down, staring at her messages. "Okay, great! Dice said he's busy tomorrow, but that he's keen to meet you in a Secotier dungeon the next day."

Frank felt confused as he got his breath back. "Why does it have to be a Secotier dungeon?"

Tessa shrugged. "It's just where he wants to do it. You can't have your stuff stolen in Secotier, remember?" Her eyes narrowed as though slightly puzzled by the name she was reading. "Have you heard of the Broken Clock Tower before?"

Frank shook his head, helmet rattling. "No."

It sounds ominous enough.

"Me neither." Tessa shrugged. "It must have been a part of the last expansion. According to the map he sent me, it's a Secotier dungeon that's on the Yarburn coast, further down the bay on the gorge's grassland. Oh well, now you two have a place to meet and make the trade."

Frank sighed, feeling like Tessa was rushing him a little, but if it was rushing him toward something he wanted, he had nothing to complain about.

I'm not gonna lie. Fifty thousand Moola is going to be really helpful. I can't wait to buy a mount that can carry a Heavy.

Chapter 7
Taking Stock

I stalked from the auction house. Knowing that Wona might once again be hunting my friends and me, I pulled up my inventory and was displeased with what I saw. I was running low on Crystal Blades, the key weapon in my arsenal. My entire strategy revolved around being able to quickly regenerate them while in a fight. With only a dozen left, I knew I would have to do some more grinding in Lucineer to restock.

More time in that frozen hell. Heck, if I'm not spending my Moola to bid on the Transfer Orb, there has to be an easier way of dealing quick damage to enemies with light weapons.

I remembered my fight against Sirswift's team during their ambush in Rubik's Castle. Sirswift had revealed that he had been Bitcon, the one I believed had kidnapped Sue, and that his team had instigated the crash that got me stuck in the game and killed her.

I also recalled the horror of seeing my Crystal Blades simply shattering against their armor. There had to be a better weapon I could use and an ability that worked to the same effect when using my Gravity Well and Speed Amp combination.

"Noah! David's gone to bed. No surprise after his last few night shifts, but I'm still up for a bit of grinding if you're up for it."

I turned to see Brock catching up to me. It was because of him that I had gotten out of Sirswift's trap alive. Because of him I didn't slip into a coma like they had hoped. He was a true friend, one I would trust both in-game and IRL, even if it was somewhat his fault Sue was dead.

"You were there, watching for the right time to swoop in and save me when I was fighting Sirswift, right?" I asked.

He nodded. "I would have used my mount's Ice Breath to do it sooner, but you used Wildfire on him. It would have countered my attack and it's a one-off kind of thing. Wipes out the rest of your Mana, too."

"Then you saw how useless my blades were against them?"

He inclined his head. "You would expect that from swords made of ice."

I looked into the New Calandor equipment stores as we passed them, window shopping. "I need a light weapon, something a bit sturdier than my Crystal blades. You know of anything like that?"

"Sure, there are tons of light swords out there. The only problem is that the lighter the weapon, the more likely it's going to break, and you won't be able to regenerate them quickly like you can with the Ice Regeneration ability."

I never realized how misleading that name was until now. It doesn't really regenerate my Crystal Blades considering it takes one of them each time I use it. Is that just the cost of summoning them quickly?

I stopped when seeing another forge, which through the curly-framed windows looked well overstocked with swords. An idea came to me then, or maybe it was a possibility.

"Brock, is there an ability like Ice Regeneration, but for regular swords?"

Brock grinned, but it was half-hearted. "Sure, but it would cost a lot of Moola to buy enough swords to use it . . . oh . . . you're going to ask us for the Moola we received from Pirate Cove, aren't you?"

I nodded sheepishly. "Just yours. If you don't need it, that is."

"Hah, ten thousand is a lot of Moola. I'll consider it your birthday present."

"Thanks, man." I gave him a friendly punch on the shoulder and we continued walking to the fountain at the city's center. "So what about this ability?"

Brock breathed in through his bared teeth. "It's called Instant Reforge. But that's the tricky part, the dungeon you have to complete to get it . . . let's just say it's an extreme environment."

"Considering I would have to spend two days in a frozen wasteland to get enough Diamond Dust to synth for Crystal Blades, completing one dungeon in an extreme environment doesn't seem like a bad alternative."

"That's because you've never been to Sulfur Pit before." Brock's eyes widened as though in pity of my naivety. "It's a Secotier dungeon between Galrinth and the Lucineer mountains better described as the dungeon closest to hell."

I suddenly recalled Data telling me of the dungeon that could be used to get to the Penance Peaks without a mount.

"Every great game should have a lava level," he had said.

I grabbed out my blue Summoning Stone. "Sounds good, let's go."

"Nope," Brock said, shaking his head. "Nope, nope, nope. We're going to Onjira first."

I made a face, and Brock laughed. "There's no talking yourself out of this one."

"You're beginning to sound just like Data."

Brock's eyes became cold. "That's not funny."

We stopped at the Gateway beside the fountain. The thing was statuesque, covered in cherubs and other old Christian iconography. The map and setting options appeared, but I was still waiting for Brock to explain why we were heading to Onjira.

"Look, Sulfur Pit is hot, and I mean extremely hot. If you just rush in there, it's unbearable. But if you spend an afternoon in Onjira, your temperature tolerance would make the heat . . . more bearable."

That's why Data was talking about Sulfur Pit when we were in Onjira. Is that the reason such a miserable place is so popular?

I nodded. "Alright fine, Onjira it is then."

We both selected Onjira and vanished from the cool streets of New Calandor, appearing in the hot winds of the desert. Dust blew in our faces and shadows of large cats and rhinos moved in the shadows of the sandstorm. It brought me back to when training here with Data a month ago. There was only one difference, my company.

"We'll head to Ayer's Rock!" Brock called, equipping his goggles. "It's the hottest place in Onjira. A few hours there should be enough."

I equipped my own goggles to block the sand. "Too bad."

Brock turned to me in confusion and I grinned at him. "I forgot my sunscreen."

Brock shook his head, grinning at the bad joke before heading off. Unlike when I headed to the rainforest with Data, the wind was at our backs. Ayer's Rock was south of the Onjira Village and was, as its name suggested, a massive sandstone monolith that looked more akin to an orange mountain than any rock.

"This place is like one giant bird coop," Brock called, lowering his voice now that the storm had calmed to a gentle breeze. "The strongest avian monsters are here. You'll be able to train up your wind and lightning magic."

"Good. I have level two spells for my earth, ice and water magic, and a level three spell for my fire magic, so it's about time my wind and lightning spells caught up."

Brock took out his white Summoning Stone. "Let's get mounted up."

I grinned. I had been waiting for a chance to ride Peragon again. Spending hours flying over the countryside and taking in the views was one of the many fond memories I had when living here.

I pulled out my own Summoning Stone and threw it into the clear blue sky. It glowed in blue pulses and with a sudden flash of white luminance, the lightning blue part-lion, part-Pegasus, part-dragon appeared where the item had been.

Brock threw his own stone in front of him and his Ice Dragon appeared before Peragon flew down next to it and we both mounted up.

"I've been meaning to ask, can all mounts use attacks like your dragon's Ice Breath?"

Brock nodded as he got comfortable between the icy edges of his dragon's plated skin. "If you look at your mount's stats, you'll see that it has something called a Loyalty Gauge. The gauge increases the more you ride or fight on them, and once it fills up completely you get to use their attack."

I looked at Peragon's stats and saw that, after all of the flying around the Dream State I did the last time I was here, the gauge was only just over the two thirds mark. "We'll be fighting avian monsters, right? Wouldn't it be easier to fight them while mounted?"

Brock smirked. "My thoughts exactly. Come on!"

Both my Peragon and Brock's Ice Dragon flapped their wings and we rose up into the hot air. We flew high into the bright sky. Brock wasn't kidding, the place was scorching. Luckily the amazing size of Ayer's Rock and all the flying monsters to hunt there took our minds off of our discomfort.

I bet it's cooler for Brock, having a massive ice sculpture between his legs.

"There are three different types of birds atop Ayer's Rock," Brock explained as we began to soar over it. "The closer to the center we get, the stronger they become. These . . ." He pointed to the cluster of small birds with fluttering wings and needle-sharp beaks. "Are the least powerful but the most annoying. Those beaks can be painful."

"We should do them at a distance then."

I raised my hand above my head and thought of a line of light forking down from the sky. A bolt of electricity struck the flock, taking out two of them and causing the rest to fly toward us. I blew them back with a Wind Blast as Brock drew out two arrows and took them down.

They vanished in puffs of feathers and dropped Resource

Items that drew toward us.

— ACQUIRED 'HUMMINGBIRD NEEDLE' —

"I would introduce the next bird, but you can see it already for yourself." Brock pointed down to the rock to see a group of large, bald birds perched around the corpse of a Mountain Lion.

"Ah, Scavenger vultures." I launched two more Lightning Strikes down on the Scavengers. "But wait, there's no way that one of those things could have carried a full grown lion all the way up here."

Brock nodded. "That will be from the third bird we'll find closer to the center. The Condors."

We flew further in, taking out several flocks of Humming Birds and Scavengers. As quick as the Humming Birds were, the Scavenger's attacks took far more Hit Points. I learned this firsthand when I ran out of Mana from using too many Lightning Strikes and one of them took a gash out of my palm.

"Son of a . . ."

Brock shot me with a specialty arrow and my Mana bar filled up. I blew it back with a Wind Blast before turning it into a roast vulture with another flash of lightning.

— WIND UPGRADE: LEARNED 'CYCLONE' —

As always when learning a new spell, a window popped up of a blank avatar showing the spell gesture while saying 'Think of wind'. Instead of one hand sweeping in front of it like with Wind Blast, the avatar had two hands outstretched, its palms rolling over one another.

"Hah, nice! That's the second time one of your arrows

saved my butt!"

By hitting my ankle during my desperate fight against Bitcon, he had caused me to fall from the Rubik's Castle's top floor just in time for him to catch me on his Ice Dragon.

Brock lowered his bow and wiped his brow. "There's something about attacking someone with good intentions that's rather satisfying. Alright, the higher we go from this point the hotter it is. It's also a good way of avoiding the Condor's first sweeping attack."

I nodded and rode Peragon further up into the sky. It was obvious Brock had done this part before, for as soon as we came to the center of the massive rock, a giant bird eclipsed the sun from above us. Even for a condor it was huge, with a long neck and a wingspan like that of an albatross. It spun and swooped below us, striking out at where we would have been.

"Attack it now!" Brock called.

With my Mana recently replenished, I did just that. Forks of lightning and exploding arrows flew down on it in a barrage that took out more than two thirds of its health before it caught on to our ambush. It spun again, shockingly quickly for such a big bird, and flew up to meet us. Its beak was long and sharp and I could see how it managed to carry the lion up this high. We dodged around it as it charged at us, spinning with another volley of magic and projectiles before . . .

—LIGHTNING UPGRADE: LEARNED 'PLASMA BEAM'—

And that's the second one down!

Deciding to test out my new spell, I followed the tutorial's instructions and cupped my hand to my waist until it started to glow the same blue as Peragon's coat. I then pushed out my hand with my index finger extended. A beam of lightning shot from it, piercing the Condor right through its breast.

Peragon spun with me as I watched it nosedive to the top of Ayer's rock. Brock and I followed it down. We were both sweating profusely by this point, but it wasn't until the fun was over that I noticed how overheated I felt. I honestly thought I was going to faint from exposure when we landed and I jumped down.

Brock walked to where the bird had landed. It vanished in a swirl of feathers, leaving one large black feather standing upright and glowing where it had been. He picked it up and grinned.

"I can synth this and the needles we received from the Humming Birds to make some decent arrows."

I raised an eyebrow at him, causing a bead of sweat to fall down my cheek. "I thought we were only here to increase my tolerance to hot temperatures?"

Brock shrugged, making the Resource Item vanish into his inventory. "Two birds, one stone."

I laughed, but not because we had just been fighting birds. It was because those were the exact same words Data had said to me after I had exited the Penance Mines with Siena. Despite their mutual dislike of each other, the two were more alike than they would ever admit.

Chapter 8
Sulfur Pit

Despite the agony of moving around in my weak body, hiding out at David's apartment was good fun. We stayed up all night eating junk food and catching up on old times. Although I knew my mother would be worried sick when she heard that I was missing from the rehab center, I also knew I couldn't tell her where I was because of the risk that she would let it slip to Wona.

By the next day, Brock had deemed my tolerance to heat stat just high enough to do the Sulfur Pit. Unfortunately, David had insisted on accompanying us without the necessary preparation. Now that I was sleeping on the couch in his room, he couldn't help but overhear and was keen to join us after I'd told him about our plan.

"I keep telling you, David. You won't be able to handle the heat!" Brock warned as we walked across the Galrinth fields just north of Lucineer.

David shrugged his heavy shoulders. "Are you kidding? It's a hundred degrees Fahrenheit outside right now, I think I'll be able to handle it."

Despite regretting not bringing David with us to train on Ayer's Rock, it was good to have the three musketeers together in a game again. It brought back memories of playing old MMOs back in high school.

Just like old times.

The lower vertebrae of the spine that made up the Alps loomed above us. The grass was soft beneath us, the southern breeze was cool and my spirits were high. I knew I should make the most of it before we entered the dungeon and found out whether the time we spent in Onjira was worth the effort.

The nostalgia made me zone out of the conversation for a moment, but I snapped back to the argument when Brock finally relented.

He rolled his eyes. "Whatever floats your boat."

"Are you sure we should let him—"

"He'll find out for himself," Brock interrupted, eyes narrowing at our Heavy. "I'm actually interested to see how long he lasts after we enter."

I recognized the entry into the mountain. It was as far north as I had gone during my training in the Lucineer tunnels before heading back to the Ice Fields. I knew there were passages in the mountain that I hadn't explored, but had no idea that they led to the Gateway of a Secotier dungeon.

Brock led the way through as David's heavy boots sunk deep into the snow at our feet. Water dripped from frozen stalactites above us.

"I don't know what you guys are on about," David said. "This place is practically a freezer."

Brock rolled his eyes. "This isn't the dungeon." He quickened his pace. "We need to hurry, before our heat tolerance lowers."

We strode further in until we saw a red glow in the darkness, the glow of a Gateway.

I pointed. "Does that one lead to Sulfur Pit?"

Brock nodded and moved ahead. "Quickly, select the Gateway!"

We did and with a flash we entered hell. The heat felt like we were inside an oven and from the smell it was cooking rotten eggs. I looked around. We stood at the start of a black-stone pathway. On either side of it was a river of magma, thick bubbles popping and wafting waves of hot air our way.

Brock grinned in David's direction. "How we feeling, buddy?"

"I've . . . been in . . . saunas . . . hotter than this." David breathed, already red in the face and dripping with sweat. "But then . . . I wasn't . . . wearing armor . . . in them."

"Don't push yourself too hard, David," I said as I started walking, determined to finish this dungeon off as quickly as possible. "You can't die in here, but the mental strain might end with you waking up with your bed soaked through with sweat."

"I'm . . . fine. Let's just . . . get this . . . over with."

It seemed to get even hotter the further we went in, if that was possible. Fire Salamanders crawled along the ceiling as serpents that seemed to be made of iron swam in the molten rock. I didn't want to waste time fighting them, no matter what Resource Items they provided. I recalled Data telling me about this place, how it made an extreme environment like the Onjira desert seem like Yarburn's tropical breeze.

From the stalactites and stalagmites to the river of magma, the entire place was either in a state of diamond hardness or liquefaction. The fact that anything could live here showed the level of fiction the game creators were willing to stretch to.

I can't believe Data was going to make me go through this place to get to Rubik's Castle. Maybe he thought having to walk through here would prevent me from attempting such a suicide mission.

"We have to make it to the caldera!" Brock yelled as though to wake himself up. "That's where the boss is. You'll have to defeat it to get the Instant Reforge ability."

David nearly fell over from heat exhaustion. Even his puffy face made him look like he was getting dehydrated. "Is that . . . why we're here?"

I nodded. "It was either that or spend a week in the Ice Fields, but as you know, we don't have a week. This is the best alternative in the time we have."

"Surely . . . you could just . . . get another staff?"

"I don't want my speed stat I put so much effort into going to waste." I gestured to Brock. "Along with—"

"Look out!"

I halted just in time to watch a Fire Salamander land in front of me. A line of flames blew from its mouth, and I countered instinctively, using my new Cyclone spell by rolling my palms around one another. A sudden rush of cool air spiraled around us, not only blowing the fire away from our path, but allowing a refreshing breeze to stop us from melting like everything around us.

As though refreshed by the wind, David ran forward and squashed the glowing lizard with his mace, smearing Red Goo on the black rock.

— ACQUIRED 'RED GOO' —

David turned back to us with a big, dumb grin on his face.

"Why didn't you do that before?" he asked.

"I thought the wind from my magic was the same temperature as whatever air surrounded us." I turned to Brock, who shrugged. "Did you know that we could use it to cool us down?"

Brock shook his head in amusement. "Although I did always think it was strange that this place was so unbearably difficult for a Secotier dungeon. Now I know why. There's an easier way to do it."

David laughed. "Well, at least using it will make it more bearable for me. Brock, shoot him up with some Mana and I'll do my Heavy stuff."

Brock did just that and I used another Cyclone to cool us down as we proceeded through the volcano toward the caldera. Feeling a lot better, I used my Ice Coffin spell to turn the Salamanders that dropped into our path to stone, allowing us to collect the Red Goo that was their Resource Item.

Even when one of the Lava Snakes attacked us, we worked together to defeat it. As it reared its gray head from the magma, I used a Gravity Pull to slow it down while Brock fired an Ice Arrow at the area around it, turning the lava to rock and trapping it in place. By that point, all David had to do was bat it around a bit before it shattered to pieces.

"David, collect those shards. You can synth them into some pretty good armor if you get enough of them."

David went about collecting them, but soon realized

that going so far away from us stopped the coolness of my Cyclone spell and he soon returned to our side. "I'll get them later, eh?"

Brock almost laughed and I was left wondering if he told David that on purpose.

Picking on David like that, no wonder he got a little fed up with him back during school.

We eventually found a passage that led us into the volcano's crater, known as the caldera. Inside the pit the brimstone was scattered with ash and large crevices had been created from the streams of molten rock.

I recalled what Data had told me about Secotier dungeons while in the Druids' Keep with Siena. He had said that if a dungeon was hard then the game designers would balance it out by making the boss less difficult. However, after learning the secret of using the Cyclone spell, the dungeon had been a cake walk and I wondered what we might be up against.

"What are we dealing with in terms of bosses here?" I asked.

"Czernobog," Brock started. "In Slavic folklore, he's the god of darkness, but you'd probably remember him as the giant monster from Fantasia. Just imagine that but held together by lava and I think you'll get the picture."

"I mean, is it strong?"

Brock nodded. "Oh yeah, one of the strongest Secotier bosses."

I didn't like the sound of that. The Dark Warrior was supposed to be a difficult Secotier boss and Data, Siena and I together had a lot of trouble with him.

Suddenly the crater began to shake around us and we stopped to balance ourselves.

"Here we go," David said, raising his mace. "I'm so ready!"

Chapter 9
Old Friends

From the caldera of the Sulfur Pit arose Czernobog. Ash came together and condensed into thick boulders. Lava then shot to the surface of the pit and linked the boulders together to form the monster, including its thin arms and legs, its spinal column and the details on its hideous skull-like face. It was like a skeleton made of rock and lava.

It arched its back and roared like it was gargling lava, and I wouldn't be surprised if it had been. The thing must have been twelve-feet-tall, but it quickly revealed how irrelevant its starting size was as it swung out one massive arm.

"Dodge!" Brock screamed.

I jumped back as the boulder flew toward David, the lava extending its limb. I dodged it, but David wasn't so lucky and it was only thanks to his thick armor that he didn't lose half of his Hit Points from the blow.

Brock fired an Ice Arrow in retaliation, hitting its extended limb and turning it to stone. I followed suit, casting Ice Wall in front of David before it could strike at him again.

The wall severed its other arm, but more lava rose from the pit and reconnected the boulders.

"That's it!" David yelled as he got to his feet and charged at the boss.

He swung his mace as the first boulder hurtled toward him, and then hit the next, aiming for Czernobog's gruesome face. Before it could hit, Brock fired another Ice Arrow, taking out its leg. David missed and jumped back as another limb extended and rushed toward him. He hit the dirt as the lava stream passed over his head.

"Use another spell!" he cried.

I noticed the crevices in the ground. "Okay, I've got an idea! Hang tight!"

I equipped my Cursed Druid Staff to increase my magic's power and found the spell I was looking for in my Key Triggers. It was there, as always.

I raised and lowered my arms in the direction of Czernobog. Gravity Well's warping vortex animation appeared over the lava monster, dragging the molten rock to the floor of the caldera and between the trenches.

"Now David! Smash that ash!"

"You got it!"

He struck his mace down on the first boulder that made up its thigh, cracking and returning it to the ash it had emerged from. Brock fired an Explosive Arrow at the boulder that made up its other thigh. When the gravity spell ceased, Czernobog rose again without legs, its torso stuck to the caldera as it used its arm to support itself.

One boulder flew at me and I hit it with a Wind Blast before a Crystal Sword flashed into my grip and I stabbed into it. I then launched a Fire Weave into the ice shards, causing it to explode like the rest.

Brock fired another arrow at me and I saw my Mana shoot back up. "Once more, Noah!"

I cast another Gravity Well and a window popped up in my vision:

— GRAVITY UPGRADE: LEARNED 'GRAVITON' —

This was followed by a window showing a blank avatar slamming his hand to the ground. *You're kidding? Alright!*

David picked off one shoulder as Brock picked off another, leaving only the head remaining. I pulled my hand back and shot a Plasma Beam from my finger to finish it off. It blasted into a cloud of ash and the lava that made up the Czernobog retreated back into the volcano from where it came.

A scroll unrolled with a trumpeted fanfare:

— DUNGEON COMPLETE —

"Oh yeah, that was way easy!" David called.

I couldn't help but laugh after our relief. *When I returned to the game, I said I would only do one dungeon and that was it. Man, was I fooling myself or what? This is so much fun. Either way, I'm here for a reason.*

I turned to Brock. "Okay, so where do I get the Instant Reforge ability?"

Brock gestured to the core of the caldera where the pit of lava bubbled. "Over there, and you're not going to like what you have to do to get it."

I suddenly remembered how I received the Ice Regeneration ability. "Let me guess, I have to put my arm in lava."

Brock nodded grimly. "So I've heard."

I stalked over to the pit, looking down the river of lava below. "Alright, let's see if Ice Coffin will do the job."

I launched the spell twice but to no effect, gesturing to Brock for assistance. He cast a few Ice Arrows down into the pit but they didn't do any more than my own spells. I realized then that I must need the level three ice spell to have any effect.

Or the equivalent powered Ice Attack . . .

"Brock, summon your Ice Dragon!"

Brock grinned. "Ah yes, I think I see what you're getting at." He then slapped his forehead. "Now that I think about, using this could have made that battle a whole lot easier, but I guess it's a good thing I didn't, considering the attack can only be used once per dungeon."

He brought out his white Summoning Stone and summoned his Ice Dragon. Mounting it, he flew high above the pit, and spending the last of his Mana, used its attack, Ice Breath. The icy wind blew down into the pit, more than enough to turn the entire surface into solid stone.

"Alright, good job!" I shouted.

Without hesitating, I jumped down onto the cooled rock and walked out over the crust. Hot jets of steam rose from the edges and cracks were slowly forming around where I stepped. It wasn't taking my weight very well.

"How is it down there?" David asked.

"You're welcome to come down and see for yourself!" I called back.

"I'm good, thanks."

Looking for a sign of where I could get the ability, I noticed something in the stone. Cast in the center of it was an unmistakable symbol, a sword. Curiously, I bent down and touched it.

— ABILITY TO LEARN 'INSTANT REFORGE' UNLOCKED —

The movement the avatar showed was almost exactly like my Ice Regeneration ability, except the drawing motion was from hip rather than over the back.

Hah! Now I just need to go sword shopping. I stood and summoned Peragon to carry me out of the pit. *Maybe Siena would know a good place. She's a Warrior after all.*

The crust I was standing on suddenly cracked like ice over a lake and steam rushed up at me. I jumped onto Peragon's back and we shot from the pit up to where David and Brock were waiting, shifting nervously from a sudden tremor that rocked the mountain.

"It's building up pressure!" Brock shouted and pulled out his Transfer Orb. "The crust is acting like a cork, we have to get out of here before it pops! Come on!"

I flew down to him and dismissed Peragon as David grabbed Brock's shoulder. We then vanished from the volcano's crater and appeared on the grass slope outside the mountain. Losing our feet on the slope, we rolled to a stop as the three of us breathed heavily from the rush of everything.

David then snorted and we all cracked up laughing. At that moment, being in the game and laughing with my best friends, it felt really good. Like nothing had changed in the years we had been apart. It was an illusion and I knew it only helped to make me forget about why I was here, to avenge Sue.

When we calmed again, Brock began talking. "You know, I was one of the beta testers of the first version of the Dream State."

David sat up. "What, but—?"

"I was a later test subject. After they had ironed out some of the kinks in the game play." His chest rose and fell on the grass. "Some of the people that died were actually on my team when testing out the digital version of the Dream State. That's what a lot of people don't understand. The Dream State was a computer game before it was a Dream Game."

From how close it resembled an MMO, even I could have guessed that much.

Brock continued. "I spent a year testing the game with them, that's what beta players are supposed to do, after all. When they asked who wanted to be the first to try out DSD and do it for real, we jumped at the chance. Almost everyone on my team died or became so mentally unstable that they couldn't defend themselves against Wona's accusations. Although Data joined our team much later, he and I are the only ones with enough mental capacity to get the evidence to bring them to justice."

His grudge against Data and his dedication to taking Wona down suddenly made a lot more sense to me. After we had left school I had mostly been with Sue and David had been hopping from one job to another before trying out the Dream Engine. Brock had made an entirely new group of friends here, and then he had lost them.

"We'll get the orb, Brock," I said. "You can count on

that."

And I'll use it to avenge Sue.

Brock stood up and the high wind brushed through his blonde hair. "With your friends helping, Noah, I think you might be right."

I stood and David followed me up.

"Well, we won't get it back by just staying here!" he called, punching the air and running down the slope onto the grasslands. "I'm starving, Noah! There's this great take-out place down the road from us that you'll love!"

I nodded and we headed down the hill after him, ready for our hunt tomorrow

The next day Siena messaged me early to meet her in Toena. I fondly recalled the Asian inspired design of the city with its tall red pagodas, Foo dog statues, and male and female NPCs in kimonos and samurai armor.

As usual Siena appeared by my side in an instant, as though she had used a Transfer Orb and Data's player-tracking software all at once. She beamed at me and placed a slender hand on my shoulder.

"So you're finally moving onto steel. I wondered how long it would take before you saw the superiority of *real* close combat. Too bad you didn't choose the right Niche. You would have made an excellent Warrior, Noah."

I rolled my eyes. "I'm a battlemage, I like to keep my options open."

Siena nodded. "A nice way of admitting to yourself

that you're a coward. Maybe if you decide to make another account then."

Shrugging, I moved down the pathway. "It's a habit I guess, considering I had a very good reason to be afraid during the time I was in here. It kept me alive."

"I guess . . ." Siena trailed off and gestured to the shopping square. "So you said you wanted to buy some light blades that were also durable. Well, this is your best bet, Wakizashi, the best in the Dream State."

"Which one?"

She pointed. "The old woman over there."

I nodded and moved over to the small forge, remembering how I had received my red Dragon Arm gauntlet from an old man here. For Primatier dungeons it was useful, but now that my robes were all the magic protection I needed, I barely had reason to use it anymore.

I arrived at the counter and pointed at the Wakizashi with a dragon engraved onto the blade. "I want a dozen."

"Whoa!" Siena called. "Big spender over here. Make it rain, Noah!"

The Wakizashi weren't cheap, which I could only attest to Siena's honesty of their quality. I knew Data knew more about equipment than her, but I felt I was on better speaking terms with Siena considering she wasn't accusing me of being a liar.

"You can also wield two at a time, and I know how much you love to dual wield, you ambidextrous son of a—"

"You sound jealous." I equipped one, holding it out and studying the long Chinese-style dragon engraved on it. "You shouldn't, after all you have one of the Color Blades."

Siena sighed. "Yeah . . . but do you know what would be

better than one Color Blade?"

"Two Color Blades?"

Siena grinned and nodded. "At the same time!"

I shook my head. If someone were to ever say that Siena could be content being one of the best players in the game, that someone wouldn't know Siena very well.

I made the short sword vanish and nodded. Now I was ready for whatever we might run into on our hunt for the Transfer Orb.

Siena raised her brow at me. "You ready?"

I nodded. "I hope so, but I guess we'll find out soon enough."

Chapter 10
The Hunt

Thanks to Siena's proposed leadership for our group, there was an unsteady truce between Data and Brock. Although it took a while for him to turn up, Data arrived with his item tracking software just as he had promised.

Without saying a word, he appeared in the Chevalier Café where we had all arranged to meet and moved over to Siena. "I'm transferring a copy of the software and the crack for installing it to you now."

She nodded and stared off into space for a moment while she accessed it. Data looked at Chloe and Keri who had decided to come with us alongside David. He looked to Brock last, who had been leaning against the back of a leather chair and glaring at him the entire time.

"Siena has promised you that she won't show me the number, I take it?" Data asked.

Brock shook his head. "Not me." He pointed in my direction. "Him."

I nodded. "Siena is someone we can trust as a neutral

party on this mission."

"If that's the case . . ." Data's eyes narrowed. "I didn't want to tell you in a message unless someone would find it, and although it's suspicious, I don't think it proves anything . . . but . . ."

"Just spit it out already!" Chloe called.

"Any unauthorized use of the item tracking software will be immediately tracked and recorded."

We all looked at each other, eyes wide.

"It's a risk we'll have to take," I said. "It's the only way to find who has the item. I can only hope they're willing to giv—"

"Alright, it's ready," Siena interrupted. "Brock, it's your turn, send me the item code number."

"You already have it."

Siena stared into space again and nodded, as though impressed. "That's definitely the item code for a Transfer Orb."

Brock frowned in confusion. "What do you mean?"

"All Transfer Orbs start with an E4 code. If you know the code, with a little programming you can trick the system into thinking you have one and use it to . . ." She stopped and looked around as though she had said too much.

"Wait a minute, is that how you appear wherever you want to?"

Siena put her hands up when seeing Data scowling at her. "I didn't say nuttin', and would you look at that, I found out where the item is!"

"Where is it?" Keri asked, as though anxious to be away from such a tense conversation.

Siena narrowed her eyes. "Hang on, he's just vanished."

"Vanished?" Brock asked, his voice showing how on edge he was.

"He must have used a Gateway . . . and there he is. He just showed up in Yarburn." Siena's eyes widened and she pulled back. "He must be late for something because he's moving pretty quickly for a Heavy."

"How do you know he's a Heavy?" Chloe asked.

"Because it says it right here." She gestured to thin air. "Name: FranktheTank, Niche: Heavy. From his stats, he looks like a bit of a newbie. Must have come across our orb by accident. Hah, what are the chances?"

She grinned but then looked up and saw our serious expressions. She returned her gaze to the map only she could see.

"He's heading out of the village to the coast. Looks like he's making a beeline to . . ." One of her eyebrows rose. "The Broken Clock Tower?" Her gaze shot to Data. "Have you heard of that dungeon before? I haven't. Is it a new one?"

Data also looked puzzled. "Tsh, the Broken Clock Tower? But that's only an experimental dungeon the engineers haven't fully worked out the mechanics for yet. The time manipulation in it is . . ." His eyes widened in what seemed like panic. "Oh crud!"

Data suddenly vanished from the bar. We all looked at each other in confusion. I felt suddenly suspicious.

"Why is FranktheTank walking to the clock tower when he has a Transfer Orb that could teleport him there?"

Siena shrugged. "Maybe he's afraid someone will see him use it and track him down. In any case, it looks like that's where we're heading. Brock, you ready?"

"When you are," he replied, sounding more jovial now

that Data wasn't around. "Ready everyone?"

We all nodded and selected the area Brock had chosen: Yarburn–Coastline. We vanished from the bar and appeared on the outskirts of the Yarburn forest, staring at a field that stretched out over the coastal gorge.

In the distance, I saw a single fully armored Heavy. He was walking quickly toward a stubby old building of brick and mortar with a huge broken clock face standing before a plateau.

So that's the unlucky fellow who found the orb?

We watched from the shadows of the swaying trees as the armor-plated giant entered the building from a broken window. I was about to chase after him but Brock held me back.

"Wait . . . look."

In the fields before the tower, seven dark figures appeared in bright flashes. The one in the middle was wearing a hood with what looked like horns sticking from it. My hackles rose and my blood roiled in my veins when I realized who they were.

Data wasn't lying. Seems we're not the only one on the hunt for this guy. Still, I was hoping I wouldn't have to deal with these bastards.

It was Bitcon and his team of miscreants, Wona's very own in-game death squad.

"Oh crap," Chloe muttered.

David nodded. "That's not good."

Siena grinned wide. "What are you talking about, this is great! We can finally get some revenge, eh Noah?"

I nodded, watching all seven of them running into the building. "In either case, we should get going now, before they realize why we're tracking him."

Although odds are they already know. But what was with Data's reaction when hearing that this was the dungeon we were heading to?

Chapter 11
The Broken Clock Tower

It wasn't just the Broken Clock Tower, it was the buried clock tower. It rose out of the earth, mostly buried like the Statue of Liberty from *The Planet of the Apes* movie. However, it looked more like Big Ben than a lady holding up a torch.

Frank had followed Tessa's directions and arrived there just after lunch. He came upon the dungeon where he was to meet with Dice. Being deep underground, it would have seemed like a good place to corner someone, but it was a Secotier dungeon where players couldn't steal items, so he couldn't think of the motive for choosing such a spot.

A simple trade, Moola for Transfer Orb. Nothing to worry about.

He stepped up onto a boulder and through a broken window in the clock face. As soon as he entered, there was the sound of gears moving and suddenly one of the hands shuddered to life, the minute hand moving from one-thirty-four to one-thirty-five. He moved further in, gazing at the sudden motion of spinning gears and pulleys moving up and down.

Frank put his speed to use and began padding down the many loose wooden stairs to the eleventh floor, seeing stenciled numbers on each of the platforms. Even after he had gone down a few floors, he still hadn't come across, or even seen, any monster encounters, let alone other players

Pretty strange dungeon. Best get in and out quickly.

He continued down a few more floors before hearing glass being broken above him, and the sounds of heavy boots on the platform above. He looked up to see a group of seven robed avatars moving in front of the giant clock face. It was the most ominous sight Frank had ever seen in the Dream State. He picked up his pace, making it to the fifth floor. The group above must have heard his descent as they began to follow him down.

The minute hand clanged and the gears around Frank rattled. He looked up to see if they were gaining on him. He felt suddenly confused when he saw that only four of them were chasing him down, the other three were running in what seemed like slow motion on the seventh floor.

Wait a minute, the clock says one-thirty-seven and they stopped on the seventh floor. Does that mean that whatever number the minute hand stops on, the players on that floor get slowed down by some kind of time magic?

He didn't have time to contemplate this. Every dungeon had some kind of gimmick, but messing with time was something Frank had never heard of. The four that were still running had started jumping floors instead of running down them.

"Why the heck are you chasing me, huh?" He then murmured to himself. "It's not like they can steal my items here!"

No one answered, and so he just kept running. Although he knew they couldn't take anything from him if they did kill him, he didn't want to be late to meet the person he promised to sell the orb to. If he was killed, he would have to start again from all the way back in Yarburn and risk being frozen by the time magic.

He managed to get to the fourth floor before they caught up with him. The robed avatars moved like ghosts, leaping from place to place. He knew tanks could take a fair bit of damage and shrug it off like it was nothing, and he was lighter than most. He decided on an action to take in the moment and acted on it without hesitation.

He jumped from the ledge and fell a good three floors before he landed . . . and fell through the floor below him into the basement level, first floor.

Well . . . that wasn't fun.

Dust clouded around him and the ground shock shook him to the bone, but he was still alive, the fall damage only taking half of his Hit Points. As the cloud of debris cleared, he looked around to see that the basement room was larger than most of the other levels. He then realized he wasn't in the basement, but at the lobby, where the ground floor should have been. Yet the stencil below him said Floor 1, as though they had messed up the numbering.

To one side was a mezzanine with a high railing, and to the other was a hallway with a fire exit sign glowing above it.

How on earth does this place still have power?

He laughed at the obvious flaw in his question. He was in a fantasy world; things didn't have to make sense. Still, looking around in a panic, he found a single shadow in the darkness.

"Dice, is that you?" he asked.

The shadow moved forward and grabbed him by the rim of his helmet. "This is a trap!"

"What? How? It's a Secotier dungeon."

In what little light there was, Frank could see the figure shaking his head. "This is an experimental dungeon, which means that the parameters for it can be redefined while people are still in it. They advertised this as a Secotier dungeon but the developers can change it to whatever they want it to be whenever they wish."

"What are you saying?" He thought he already knew, but his panic made him ask all the same.

"I'm saying that this is now a Tertiatier dungeon that you are trapped inside!"

Frank's eyes widened in horror. That was why he had been chased by those robed avatars, that's why they had told him to meet Dice at the bottom—so he would be trapped.

But how did they know where to find me. Did Tessa tell them?

"That's impossible! I don't believe you!"

The form shook him. "It's true, you must face it!"

"W-what can I do?"

"There's only one thing you can do. Take a leap of faith. They're only looking for you because they know you have the orb, but they're not looking for me. Give me the orb and I swear you will get it back once you've returned to the game."

In his panic Frank didn't even think to use it himself.

"How can I know I can trust you?"

Frank could hear footsteps above them and he gasped as they walked to the hole in the floor.

"You can't. That's why it's a leap of faith."

The stranger was whispering now, showing that he wasn't with the group who was chasing him. If what he said was true, he would lose the orb anyway. At least this way there was a chance of him getting it back.

"Okay, here!" He was shocked by the fear in his voice.

He brought out the Transfer Orb and passed it over to him. The man seemed to hold the item in reverence for a second before he nodded and grasped his shoulder.

"You made the right choice. I'll be seeing you soon."

This confirmation felt only a little reassuring considering he had just given away his most precious item to a stranger. He looked up as he heard the group from above find the stairs to the lobby and begin their descent.

"So what's your name? How can I contact you?"

He turned back but the shadow had vanished. Suddenly, six trails of green flames flew across the room, each of them giving form to one of the cloaked figures who had chased him. They rose from the shadows all around him. Now he was the only one standing in the light coming in from the hole in the roof he'd made .

"Who are you? What do you want from me?"

They didn't answer him.

"If you want the Transfer Orb . . . I don't . . ."

They continued to advance on him. He knew he was a dead man, and he had just given away the one thing that could've allowed him to escape.

Why? Why can't anything go my way for once, huh?

"Just leave me alone!" he cried.

There was the sound of the minute hand turning, and like those that had been caught on the number of the floor correlating to the minute hand, he could barely move. No one in the lobby could move freely, not even the hooded men. They stepped toward him in slow motion, which actually made it slightly scarier by how helpless he was.

This is it. There goes all my equipment. Damn it!

Suddenly another hole was blown in the roof from a beam of light and a young man dropped through, falling slowly as though caught by a gust of wind. Dust flew from him and his cloak tail billowed out behind him. When the wind stopped, he landed and slammed his hand into the floor. A warping animation appeared around the entire room, slowing everyone to a near complete halt.

Silence seemed to fill the hall, and in the light of the second hole in the ceiling, the stranger stood. He looked around at the shadowed figures moving bare fractions of a second around him, and then turned to Frank with a grin.

"Hold tight, big guy," he said. "This shouldn't take too long."

He lowered his stance and spread his arms as a short sword appeared in each hand. He then seemed to vanish in a blur of speed. Frank watched as he appeared in front of one of the hooded avatars, his blades attacking from all angles before he vanished again and the avatar exploded into a particle effect. The young man reappeared with an arcing swing that struck at the top of another player's head, spinning into another barrage of attacks until that player was obliterated as well.

One after another he appeared before each of the cloaked avatars, taking them out with what seemed several precise cuts before moving onto the next. When both of his short swords broke against one of robed players, another set appeared in his hands as he continued his grim work of dispatching the team.

Frank gaped in awe as the ominous party that had been chasing him was being quickly picked apart and laid to waste by a single player sporting two short swords and who-knew-what combination of magic.

He has to be Hero rank to be this powerful!

Finally, the young man came to the last robed figure and with his final swing, took his head off at the shoulders. As soon as he did, the clock chimed, signaling that one minute was up and time for him finally went back to normal.

One minute . . . he took out the entire party in one minute!

The young man in the hood straightened and turned to Frank. "So, you're the one I've been looking for. Please tell me you still have the orb."

Dice?

He barely had time to think this before the ceiling caved in around them.

Chapter 12
Time

We quickly filed into the clock tower and looked down at the massive opening between the platforms leading twelve floors down into the earth. I felt sudden vertigo at seeing such a huge drop into the dusty ruins.

Cloaked forms rushed down the platforms after the plate-armored Heavy. From the way the scaffolding had rattled when Brock walked out onto it, I was surprised to see an avatar in full armor move so quickly down the fragile wooden steps.

The sight told me two things, the first was that Bitcon was forcing the Heavy into a trap by driving him to the bottom buried deep under the earth, and the second was that to catch up with him we would need to do something drastic.

Chloe moved back through the window as though being on a shaky platform so high up unsettled her. "I'll keep watch to make sure no one takes us in the rear."

David smirked. "Afraid of heights?"

She gave an uneven, sarcastic laugh and moved back outside as the rest of us moved down the dusty wooden planks to the tenth floor. We quickly realized that trying to catch up by running down the steps would only waste what precious time we had.

"We need a strategy," Brock said.

I shook my head. "We don't have time for a strategy."

Keri grinned. "That's something I would expect Siena to say."

Siena patted me on the back. "I'm rubbing off on you, Noah." She nodded. "He's right, though. I'll go first and you guys can take out any stragglers I leave behind."

"How?" Brock exclaimed. "You won't be able to land from this high up with your Hit Points still intact!"

"That's fine, I'll just use . . ." She frowned and squinted into thin air. "Hah, well how about that? I actually can't use it in here. That's strange . . . the only dungeons I can't use it in are . . ."

"Tertiatier dungeons," I finished for her, remembering what Data had said before vanishing. "It's obvious. They changed this dungeon to a higher tier to make it so Bitcon's team could take out Frank and steal the Transfer Orb!"

"Seriously?" David exclaimed.

"Wait! Augh . . . !" I cried out as the Heavy jumped over the railing of the fourth floor in an attempt to escape his pursuers, crashing into the basement in a plume of dust.

"They'll be able to destroy the evidence if they get their hands on it!" Brock's eyes darted as he tried to think of a way down.

"If that's the case . . ." Siena shrugged and walked to the edge of the platform. "There's only one way to get down to the bottom before they do."

Without hesitation, she grabbed hold of the platform's railing and launched herself over the edge, falling between them.

She screamed a "Woohoo!" as she dropped.

Bitcon's team had reached the bottom. Like wraiths, they moved silently to the stairs, all but one of them. Bitcon remained, his hooded form spinning as Siena reached the bottom. His hand shot out and Siena was blasted away by a wind spell. The other hooded forms spun on her but Bitcon waved them on. He then summoned his Jade Edge as Siena flipped back and summoned her Ruby Edge. They charged in, their blades clashing.

I went to follow her down but the clang of the minute hand rung out. A light flashed around us, and it was suddenly difficult to do anything.

I . . . I can't move!

My eyes swiveled sluggishly to the others, all looking as confused as we could only watch Siena and Bitcon's fight. He used several spells against her to no avail, doing more damage to the dungeon than to her. As though she had heard the noise from outside, Chloe returned to see what was going on. She ran down to the floor we had stopped on and panted when she caught up to us.

"There's no one else out there. I . . ." Her eyes narrowed at our expressions slowly becoming surprised. "Hey, why is everyone being so still?" she asked, moving freely around the platform to look into our faces.

The specific mechanics of the Broken Clock Tower suddenly made sense as the spell's hold on me wore off.

It's not the floor that casts the spell; it's the clock changing that causes time to slow. Considering the minute hand was on the ten, it correlates to the floor number. It must cycle through each floor every ten minutes! I grinned as a plan came to me, knowing I would have to risk everything to time it just right. *And after ten it will go back to one, meaning time will stop next on the ground floor!*

I turned to Chloe and the rest. "Everyone, go back up Siena. I know what I have to do. Keri, cast Speed Amp on me, I'm going to need all of the Mana I have for this."

Keri nodded, and before the minute hand could clang, I grabbed hold of the railing and followed Siena over the side. The experience of falling made my mind rush, but I knew what spells I could use to survive the landing.

Cupping my hand at my side and pointing my index finger at the floor rushing up at me, I blasted a hole right through it with a Plasma Beam. I then placed both hands out in front of me and rotated my palms around each other. The wind from my Cyclone spell caught me up and slowed my fall as I passed through the hole in the floor and landed in the dark lobby of the clock tower.

When I saw how slowly the robed figures were moving, I knew my suspicions had been correct. I planted my hand onto the floor, just as I had seen in the spell tutorial, and cast Graviton on the entire room, grinding their already slow movements to a complete halt.

I saw in my periphery that Frank was behind me now.

There you are!

"Hold tight, big guy," I said. "This shouldn't take too long."

I grinned when seeing they hadn't managed to reach him yet. Using my new Instant Reforge ability, two Wakizashi flashed into my open hands, the only swords now in my inventory. Siena had been right, I really did enjoy dual wielding.

It seemed Keri's Speed Amp spell had leveled up since I had last seen her, for even I gasped at how fast I could move. It was much more powerful than mine, that's for sure.

I appeared before the hooded forms, and with pleasure, went about dispatching Bitcon's team members one by one with quick swings of my short swords. Although annoyed that Bitcon himself wasn't among them, I felt satisfied in the assumption that some of the avatars I was cutting down were players who had been a part of the trap in Rubik's Castle. It only took breaking two of my dozen short swords to finish the job.

I almost felt disappointed when it was over, but knew as the bell rang and the spell wore off that I had been right to kill them quickly. I turned to Frank, who still sat on the floor, eyes bulging through his helmet's visor.

"So you're the one I've been looking for," I said through panting breaths. "Please tell me you still have the orb."

The Heavy seemed stunned, and before he could answer me, there was a rumble above and the ceiling fell in on top of us from one side of the hall. I rolled toward him and cast an Ice Wall behind him, stopping the planks from landing on us. Instead they boxed us in.

I cast another Plasma Beam to blast two of the boards away and looked up as flashes of green and red streaks lit the darkness of the mezzanine above us. Siena and Bitcon went head to head, their Color Blades ringing with their quick slashes and parries.

I couldn't help but stare in awe at the two flipping and

darting over each other, blades clashing. From the lights that were shining around Siena, I could see that Keri had arrived and was using her support spells to give her an edge over Bitcon.

David dropped from the roof beside me and shoved some of the debris aside to allow us up. Brock and Chloe fired arrows and threw knives in their attempt to assist Siena's melee. Bitcon blocked desperately with a shield spell and then cast a Fire Weave at Siena that filled the darkness with an orange light.

Siena flipped backward and landed beside David, Frank and I on the lobby floor. Brock, Chloe and Keri then dropped down behind us and all six of us stood protectively around Frank. Our odds were suddenly looking a lot better.

As though trying to bluff us out of our victory, Bitcon jumped up onto the mezzanine's banister, a hellish grin on his face.

"Do you even know what I am?" he asked.

"You're outnumbered is what you are!" I called back. "You can't get to him through us and you know it!"

Bitcon shook his head, flicked back his hood to show his pale elven face and began to laugh. His bellows echoed off the walls as he clutched at his gut. When he calmed, he mimed wiping a tear from his eye and even as he talked, he seemed to be holding down sniggers.

"*Get* to him?" He leered. "I don't need to *get* to him. Everything he had that we wanted is already in our possession."

My heart leapt into my throat. "What?"

I looked back at the Heavy quivering behind me.

Did Frank already give him the Transfer Orb? If that's true, why were they still trying to kill him?

Bitcon gestured out a hand, and with a flash, another man in a hooded cloak appeared and moved up to the railing to stand beside him.

"You actually thought he was your friend?" Bitcon teased as the avatar reached up and pulled off his hood.

Data looked down on us, his expression grim.

Chapter 13
Betrayal

I had to give it to Data. He'd even had me fooled. Bitcon put out his hand and Data removed something from his cloak. It was the Transfer Orb, its green glow lighting the mezzanine where they stood.

"Don't do it!" Brock called, as though thinking he could plead to the small part of Data that still remained loyal to the memory of his friends.

Chloe bared her teeth in a snarl and Keri made an expression as though her mother had just told her that Santa Claus wasn't real. David shook his head, and for the first time since I had known her, Siena looked utterly baffled.

Bitcon lowered his open hand and Data placed the Transfer Orb inside his grasp.

"Traitor!" I yelled.

"Rat bastard!" Siena called, also seeming to have her own choice words for him. "Why did you warn us we were going to be tracked, huh? Unless . . ." She quickly trailed off, eyes going suddenly distant in thought.

"So this is the orb you have all been scrambling around

trying to find, huh? The only item with the evidence that could supposedly put Wona away?" Bitcon held it aloft for all to see, so close but still out of reach. "Such a pity."

His hand clenched and he smashed the orb within his grasp, the representation of it vanishing as the video evidence of the beta tester's overdosing was deleted entirely from the game's memory. It felt like everything we had done, all we had struggled and trained for, was suddenly for naught.

"No!" Brock fell to his knees, as though driven down by the guilt of his friends dying for nothing.

I ground my teeth, two Wakizashi flashing into my hands. "You're a dead man!"

"Do you really think it matters?" Bitcon asked, gesturing to the room around us. "That you might kill me? That you took out my men? It doesn't, you know? Only the orb mattered, and now it's gone."

Siena raised her own blade and David his mace.

"You don't believe me?" Bitcon shrugged. "Let me show you then."

He flicked one arm out to the side and behind him on the mezzanine his entire team respawned, flashing back into the world as though I hadn't even killed them. I gasped as the pointlessness of defeating these people became abundantly clear to me. We were far from outmatched. We were outgamed.

"You see, Noah?" Bitcon taunted, his smile stretching his thin lips. "I can respawn any of my teammates as soon as they die, just like your swords, just like . . ." He clicked his fingers. "That."

"Hacks!" David called. "Haven't you ever heard of fighting fairly?"

"Data, how could you?" Chloe screamed. "We all looked up to you!"

I had never heard such emotion in Chloe's voice. She hadn't even been that close to Data, but it seemed she took his betrayal rather personally.

"He was Wona's loyal dog from the beginning. All it took was a little sniff for him to come running." Bitcon rolled his wrist. "And . . . as fun as it is to see the looks on your faces in the knowledge of your defeat, I'm getting a bit sick of him being the center of attention. Let's put an end to this, shall we?"

He gestured to those in his party and the robed forms leapt from the platform onto the floor around us.

"Brock, your Transfer Orb, get us out of here!" Siena whispered.

Still on his knees, Brock shook his head. "They've taken away my ability to access its Key Trigger. There's only one way we're getting out of here."

Siena grinned. "Yeah, we fight our way out!"

Chloe shook her head. "I don't think that's what he meant."

I ground my teeth as they surrounded us. "You're such a pessimist."

"The word you're looking for is realist." Chloe smirked at my side. "Although, I guess it won't be the first time I've been taken out fighting next to you, Noah."

"Me, too!" Keri called, as though it were a club she was proud to be a part of.

"It's not something to brag about!" David shouted.

Weapons arose from their cloaks as they closed in on us. Siena charged in and took out one of the Warriors without much effort. However, as soon as I took out a Spellcaster with a Plasma Beam, that same Warrior was respawned and charged in to attack us. Bitcon hadn't been lying; they really could respawn like an Instant Reforge.

"We have to run!" I called.

"Where?" Chloe asked, jumping back and tossing out her throwing knives. "We're surrounded and the floor above has caved in so we can't get to the stairs! We're stuck here!"

"There has to be something we can do!" Keri cried. "There must be some way out of here! Some way . . ."

There wasn't. I'd like to say we went down gracefully, all of us fighting to the bitter end, but to be honest, it was devastating.

For every member of Bitcon's crew we cut down, previously killed members swiftly took their place. The first to go was Brock. Having lost all hope in getting the orb back, my old friend barely even put up a fight.

Frank went quickly after. Although he was by far the weakest among us, I could at least say the Heavy fought bravely. Battered around by an enemy Heavy, he was finished off with an arrow through his helmet's visor. When he vanished, he left behind his suit of armor, uncommon to have an entire suit all of the same plate.

The next to get taken out was Chloe, which was only natural for a Range fighter in a close combat situation. After leaping back from a sword swing, she was blown to pieces by an explosion from a respawned Spellcaster. She dropped her assassin's leathers and two of the throwing knives she had been holding.

The fourth to go was David, although it took two Heavy's to finally take him out after Keri cast Enrage on him and he pulled out his battle axe. They managed to stun him with a flail as another ran him through with a Broadsword. When he disappeared, he dropped his axe as the weapon they could steal if they chose to.

With enemies generally going for the supporting mage first so that they couldn't assist their teammates, Keri lasted longer than I would've thought. However, after casting a final protection spell on Siena and another level two speed spell on me, she was severed at the waist by a passing warrior Siena must have killed several times already.

In the end, Siena and I fought back to back, just as she had always wanted. She took out the Heavies and the team's tougher Warriors while I launched spells to cut down the Range and Spellcaster avatars. Siena finally went down laughing after Bitcon trapped me in an Ice Coffin and she was left to fight all six Wanted rank players alone.

I watched from the cold prison of ice that held me as she fought like a demon. She was finally brought down by a player she'd already killed at least seven times over. It wasn't the worst way to go down, but it was hard to watch the redheaded Range Niche claim her Ruby Edge, her prized possession, after she was gone.

I can confidently say my own death was the worst of the lot. Not only did I stick around to watch all of my friends die and lose their cherished items, not only was I shattered within the ice that imprisoned me, leaving me completely helpless, but I recognized the big dumb grin of the Heavy that finally finished me off with his Morning Star.

It was the barbarian avatar Bitcon had pointed out to me in Rubik's castle, the player he claimed had been the driver of the truck that had crashed into us on his orders. I was forced awake with the knowledge that this was the second time the bastard had succeeded in screwing up my life irrevocably.

The only bright side I could find, and I really had to look hard to find one, was that the most valuable attributes of my avatar were the spells and abilities I had collected over my time in the game, and they couldn't be stolen. However, it was little solace with how easily we were defeated.

Chapter 14
Continue?

I wasn't sure what hurt more after our loss, my feeble body or my broken heart. We all arranged to meet back up outside the village of Yarburn. It seemed fitting as it was where we had gathered to do our first dungeon together only months ago. Like at the New Calandor harbor, cries of seagulls could be heard over the crashing waves, however, here the heat and smell of salt and fish was much more prevalent.

As I made my way to the beach seats that wound their way around the village wall, I realized I was the last one to arrive. Although some of us had weapons hoarded away on other accounts, I resorted to using my navy blue Silk Robes that I had synthed from Spider's Silk in Galrinth after completing the Widow's Forest with Data.

Was he working with Bitcon even then, or did he bend the knee only recently? He claimed he had no idea Sirswift was Bitcon when I mentioned it to him. Either that was true, or his time as a game salesman had taught him a little more than just promoting game mechanics.

Needless to say, we looked like a diverse group of newbies and vets brought low. Brock in particular still had his leathers and a spare bow. Despite this, he slouched against the seat looking miserable, and for a good reason. I figured by this point that most of us were thinking of giving up on the Dream State entirely, even me.

"Let's get the obvious out of way," Siena said, her tone more solemn than I was used to. It only made sense considering she had just lost one of seven rarest items in the game. "We were beaten . . . badly, and there was nothing we could have done to prevent that."

"It wasn't fair!" David shouted. "If they didn't have their administration powers we would have beaten them ten times over!"

"Maybe not that much," Chloe murmured, sounding rather sour herself.

"In any case, there's a chance to get back what we lost," Siena continued, a smile playing on her lips. "After all, I still have Data's item tracking software."

Keri's eyes widened and she smiled. "You didn't delete it?"

Siena shrugged. "Why should I? It's not like Data kept his promise to us. Besides, I plan on getting my Ruby Edge back."

"It doesn't matter!" Brock called out.

We all turned to him at his sudden outburst.

"Don't you get it? The Transfer Orb was all that could take Wona down! Without it we're just playing the game!"

"Yeah . . . ?" Siena said, as though waiting to hear his point.

Brock shook his head. "I'll play for as long as it takes

to get your equipment back, I owe you guys that much, but that's it. After that, I'm leaving the game for good. It's messed up my life enough already."

I nodded, feeling I might do the same, but I still wasn't sure how I felt about playing the game for the game itself. I had to admit that there were times where the experience provided much enjoyment, but with how personal my goals in the world had become, it also provided a whole lot of heartache.

"Considering the Ruby Edge is the most valuable item, I think we should try to retrieve that one first." I noticed Chloe frowning at me. "Also the party only had one Range Niche, that's the redhead. I don't know what his name i—"

"His name is Dice!"

We all turned to the unfamiliar brittle voice behind us and saw an avatar staring at us from down the beach, breathing heavily, as though she had rushed up to meet us. It was rare to see a female Heavy, let alone a Heavy not wearing armor. The woman had a wide frame, dark hair pulled back into a ponytail and had soft features for a giant.

"Who are you?" David asked.

The Heavy sighed as though ashamed of herself and I suddenly realized who she was.

"Frank?" I asked incredulously. "FranktheTank?"

The large woman nodded.

"But Frank's a boy's name . . ." Keri said thoughtlessly but then covered her mouth. "I'm sorry, I didn't mean to—"

"It's short for Francine, but I admit I wanted to give the idea that I was male here without having to change my gender in the game. Frank also rhymes with tank. No one likes female tanks and I guess I just got used to being considered another male tank." She looked down in sorrow. "FranktheTank was my identity here. That's all."

Chloe screwed up her face. "But why be a tank? The female designs for them aren't very flattering."

"Because tanks are awesome!" Frank exclaimed. "They're massive and can take out almost every other Niche in close combat."

Siena nodded in approval. "Good answer. So how do you know the name of the guy from Bitcon's team?"

Frank's eyes shifted. "A friend of mine told me to go meet him to trade the Transfer Orb. She said he's the only male Wanted rank with red hair."

"Well, at least we know the name of our target, but it looks like you've been looking for us." Brock gave Frank a suspicious glare. "So what do you want?"

"I figured some of you would want to get your gear back. Well, you're not the only ones. That armor was my disguise for my identity here. Without it I'm just another freakish female heavy." Frank's gaze dropped. "Besides, I don't know if I can trust the friend who told me about Dice anymore. For Pete's sake, I should have been more suspicious about a player with a name as simple as Dice!"

"Alright." I stood and gestured to Siena. "Put the item code of the Ruby Edge into the tracker and we'll see if we can ambush him in a Tertiatier dungeon."

Siena's gaze lifted, as though she was looking at the map brought up by the tracking software. She tapped the air in front of her, entering the code, but then frowned.

"Why the pout?" Chloe asked.

"Well, that's just weird." Siena repeated her actions and then frowned again, putting her hands on her hips. "I don't really know."

"Does it not show the item?" Keri asked. "This Dice guy might just be logged out."

"The opposite actually." Siena grinned in her confusion. "There must be some kind of hack put on the item because it's saying it's in four Tertiatier dungeons at once!"

Chloe leaned forward. "The heck?"

Siena pointed at her invisible window as though offended by something it was showing her. "That's what it says."

Brock stood from his seat, hands in his pockets. "We'll have to split up into groups of two to find the right location. Everyone alter your menu settings so that you can receive messages while in dungeons. If you come across Dice, message me and I'll use my own Transfer Orb to grab the others and back you up."

Chloe narrowed her eyes at him. "But there are only seven of us. That means one of us will have to go alone."

Brock grinned at her. "And you hassle me for pointing out the obvious. I'll go by myself. I'm still pretty powerful even without my best equipment."

We nodded.

"So what are the dungeons then?" I asked.

Siena started reading them off. "Cobra's Den in the Barrens north of Onjira, Diamond Hollow west of Onjira—"

"Oh, I've always wanted to go to that one!" Keri said, raising her hand excitedly before turning to David. "You should tag along, Davey. I've heard you can get some really strong armor there."

David nodded in agreement. "Sounds like we'll be taking that one."

Siena continued. "There's Ghost Town north of New

Calandor and the Ice Fortress in Lucineer."

I bobbed my head. "I did want to explore New Calandor a little bit more, so I'll do the Ghost Town one if you're all fine with that."

"You should go with him, Chloe. It's a great place for Range Niches to train up. Besides . . ." Brock inclined his head mockingly. "The smell of gunpowder might grow on you."

Chloe gave him an annoyed look but then walked over to stand next to me. "I doubt it, but I do need new weapons with my throwing knives stolen. Maybe a pair of pistols or a rifle will be just the ticket."

"That's leaves Cobra's Den and the Ice Castle," Siena raised her brow at FranktheTank. "How about it, Efty? Want to explore a giant snake pit with me?"

Efty?

Frank laughed nervously. "If it means doing a dungeon with Siena_the_Blade, I wouldn't care where I went."

She winked at her. "Another good answer. You're on a roll."

Brock turned his back on us. "That leaves me with the Ice Castle. I fortunately still have all the frost resistance I need after our excursion there."

I knew he was talking about the time we had done the Lucineer Glacier together. "Alright, good luck."

Brock nodded. "You, too."

He vanished and the rest of us began to make our way to the Yarburn Gateway down the beach.

"You need to stop looking so down, Noah." Chloe grinned proudly beside me. "This gives you a good excuse to spend some valuable one-on-one time with me."

I grinned at her and said sarcastically. "Oh, goodie."

She punched my arm and I laughed.

There were some good parts about playing this game; it all depended on the company you kept.

Chapter 15
Ghost Town

We arrived next to the fountain in New Calandor and began searching the shops for equipment we could take with us to Ghost Town. Luckily, Chloe still had her ten thousand Moola from Pirate Cove. I sold six of my Wakizashi, keeping two for an emergency. Of the four I'd had equipped in the Broken Clock Tower, two had broken and the other two had been stolen.

We moved down the black brick sidewalk. The shy smiles Chloe had been hiding became more obvious as we walked alone to the main shopping district. The face she made when I caught her doing it reminded me of her expression after she had kissed me on the Yarburn shore after Bitcon had first attacked me.

What did that even mean? Nothing came of it, after all.

We stopped outside the firearms store and I gestured Chloe in. "Ladies first."

Chloe smiled. "What a fine young gentleman you are."

She slipped up on the doorstep, catching herself in embarrassment before entering. In the store, we searched for different weapons that appealed to us. I wondered if there were any niche-crossover weapons in there. Usually such weapons could only be synthed, but this was New Calandor after all, and a player had to be able to last in a Tertiatier dungeon just to get to this place.

It only makes sense that a setting that could only be accessed by elite players would provide more advanced weaponry.

Among the revolvers and crossbows, a weapon caught my eye. It was a rifle, but one end was designed to look like a wizard's staff. *A gunstaff?*

The weapon was called a *Boomstick*. I nodded at it appreciatively and took a look at its stats. Although not as strong as my Druid's staff, it had high magic and also increased the range of whatever spells I cast.

In the demonstration window that I selected, it showed via a blank avatar how a player could launch a spell through the rifle-end to wherever the player was aiming.

Neat. What are Spellcasters but a slower, more powerful version of Range fighters, after all? Although I better not say that in front of Chloe.

I gestured the cowboy hat-wearing store clerk over to the Boomstick and purchased it with the Moola I'd received from selling my blades. I had learned my lesson from before about fighting Bitcon's team close up. His Instant Respawn ability made taking them out one at a time completely pointless.

I turned and watched as Chloe stepped out of a dressing booth. I had never been so amused and endeared at the same time before. She was wearing the cutest cowgirl getup I had ever seen, complete with vest, leather chaps, a wide brimmed hat, dual revolvers and a belt of bullets.

She narrowed her eyes at me, as though daring me to say

something bad about it. "What?"

I raised my hands. "Nothing. I just think I figured out one of the perks of making it this far up the ranks."

She blushed and turned away. Deciding to add to her wardrobe, she purchased a beige duster to make her look more like a cowgirl and less like a stripper.

I nodded. "Much better."

She rolled her eyes and turned to the desk. "Whatever."

Despite her reaction, we each walked out with our own western attire. With my own trench coat over a dark suit and pants, we made for a formidable looking duo. I grabbed the collar of my coat and pulled it tight, ready to make our way out of the city to the Gateway that led to Ghost Town.

When we walked out onto the dusty trail we saw a stable of horses. The Gateway shone on top of the horses' backs. We mounted up, and like with the ship to Pirate Cove, there was only the starting scene of our ride, merely setting off before teleporting us straight to the dungeon.

The Ghost Town was exactly what you would expect of a dungeon with that name. The place was completely desolate, not even a mule and cart were in the street. A brisk wind blew a tumbleweed across a barren hardpan road between two rows of wooden houses.

Chloe looked around, still holding onto her horse's reins. "Looks like a scene out of every western I've ever watched."

"Reminds me of the town from *A Fistful of Dollars*," I murmured as we dismounted our horses and strode in.

I looked up at the second stories of the surrounding buildings, keeping an eye out for gun barrels poking out from behind pulled curtains.

Chloe raised her brow at me. "You like that movie?"

I shrugged. "A western reinterpretation of Yojimbo, a much older Japanese film."

Chloe snorted. "I knew that . . . I was just wondering if you did." She stopped and looked up in confusion.

I followed her gaze to the end of the road. At the distant end of town was the silhouette of a tall gunslinger wearing a poncho, his shadow stretching along the dusty carriage track.

"Is that . . . ?"

She nodded. "The Man with No Name himself."

"This must be the only dungeon where you see the boss before you see his minions." I looked around, seeing no sign of anyone in the houses. "Doesn't look like Dice is here. We should message the others."

"Doesn't look like anyone's here but him." Chloe gestured to the man and smiled. "Come on, Noah. Let's at least test this guy out before we head off. This is a Tertiatier dungeon, and if this is it, this gunslinger has to be pretty badass, right?"

I inclined my head. "Let's find out."

Eager to test out my new weapon, I equipped it with a flash and aimed the barrel at the lone gunman. I then selected Wildfire in my Key Triggers and fired. The entire end of the street burst into flame, burning the edges of the houses surrounding the gunslinger black. When the momentary inferno vanished, he still stood there, untouched with smoke billowing from the ground around him.

Huh . . . nothing.

That's when I noticed his shadow shifting on the ground. Like the hand of a clock, it turned in our direction as the man removed his hand from his poncho. Recalling the many western movies I had watched, I suddenly realized what was about to happen.

"Chloe, run!"

It seemed I didn't need to tell her for she bolted for one of the houses at the exact same time as me. We moved behind one of the first wooden houses, put our backs to the wall and gasped.

The town suddenly came to life, and the double meaning of why it was called Ghost Town became inescapably clear. The ghosts of townsfolk, mothers, fathers and their dead children, began to walk out the front doors. They all wore vests, dungarees, and cross-patterned shirts, as you would expect from townsfolk in a western.

"Can we go now?" I asked.

Chloe didn't answer. She just peered around the side of the building, drew her dual revolvers and began firing. Granted, her aim was dead on, but it was like shooting . . . no it *was* shooting at ghosts. The bullets passed right through them, their translucent forms parting and stretching away to avoid their trajectory. After she had emptied her guns and spun back to reload, each of the ghosts she had shot at suddenly turned in our direction.

"Looks like you got their attention!" I called.

Chloe sat back and reloaded. "The gunslinger at end of the road is obviously the conjurer of these ghosts. We kill him, we take them all out."

"Are you just guessing or do you actually know that for sure?"

She shrugged. "Got any better ideas?"

I lifted my Boomstick and grinned at her. "Good point."

She grinned back and we both rushed around the other side of the building, moving away from the ghosts to encircle the gunslinger. His shadow followed us as we moved until we stopped behind him. The ghosts had turned in our direction and were slowly beginning to amble our way.

"He's not turning around!" Chloe called.

With a start, I noticed a barrel of another of the gunslinger's revolvers poking out behind him in our direction. On instinct, I rubbed my hand in front of me and summoned a wall of ice just in time to block his bullets.

Ice shot out in front of us as Chloe looked out from behind it and fired her own guns. There were the pinging sounds of bullets bouncing off metal as they hit him. I then recalled how, in *A Fistful of Dollars*, the Man with No Name had tied a piece of metal to his torso and taunted the villain to shoot him only in the heart.

"Aim for the head!" I yelled.

She fired her last two rounds, and this time we saw him stagger.

So he can only be hit by physical attacks and only if they're headshots. What a pedantic way to beat a boss!

I looked over the crumbling ice to see the ghosts begin to crowd around the gunslinger, passing through him on their way to us.

"I can't see him properly; the ghosts are getting in the way of my sight!" Chloe called as she reloaded her revolvers.

"I'll see what I what I can do!"

I reinforced the Ice Wall, and as I did, the gunslinger fired two more shots toward us, causing ice to explode around where I had poked my head out. As he did, the edges of the ghosts moved as if to avoid the sonic boom of the air that went around the bullets. I then remembered what had happened when Chloe had fired at them.

They phased around the bullets like the air repulsed them.

These ghosts must be weak against wind magic.

I lifted my Boomstick and took aim, selected my Cyclone spell and shot it directly at the gunslinger. Once again, the magic had no effect on the boss himself, but it did cause the ghosts around him to stretch and shift away, as though caught in the wind. It gave Chloe a clear shot.

She unloaded on the gunslinger, each one a headshot. I assumed that Range fighters used the same targeting system for both guns and other projectile weapons because there was no way she could have been that good right from the get-go. Chloe reloaded and we repeated this strategy several more times, the ghosts continuing to get closer as I blew through them again and again with my Cyclone spell before running out of Mana.

After two more shots from Chloe, the gunslinger staggered again and finally fell to his knees, dropping his own revolvers onto the dusty road. The ghosts around him then simply vanished. The two of us sighed with relief and sank against the wall of ice next to each other. Seeing how similarly we had reacted after the rush of the battle, the two of us couldn't help but laugh. We laughed until our lungs burned and all we could do was catch each other's eyes.

Like last time, Chloe's kiss was sudden, like she was trying to steal it from me before I could notice. However, this time I let her, reaching around her waist and pulling her closer. Whether it was the heat going to my head or the adrenaline pumping in my veins, just being able to do this made me feel alive again.

"Only if you don't go for Chloe during your time here, either. I won't have you putting her through something that will hurt her just because she can't communicate her feelings as well as I

can."

Keri's words during our time at the Tranquil Grotto made me pull away. Chloe looked at me panting, her cheeks flushed.

She stood quickly and turned away from me. "We should find out how the others are doing! You can check and I'll grab the Resource Item."

I nodded speechlessly and checked my messages. There were two waiting for me.

The first was from Frank: "We located Dice, but Siena decided to rush in and fight him instead of calling for backup. He got away."

Typical.

I frowned, wondering if getting the message sooner would have made a difference. However, the second message caught my attention even more, making my breath catch in my chest.

It was from Data: "We need to talk. Just the two of us. Meet me where you unlocked your first spell. Tell no one."

Where I unlocked my first spell? I know where that is, the Penance Mines, but why be so vague? My brow furrowed. *Is he afraid Wona is reading his messages? But why? Did he do something to get them suspicious? And why just me?*

I rose to my feet and Chloe turned to me, her face concerned.

"The Resource Item was just gunpowder . . . " She drew closer to me. "What's wrong?"

"Meet up with the others." I moved around her, heading back to the horses. "There's something I have to do."

Chapter 16
Forgiveness

Why did I say I would be fine with any dungeon?

The Cobra's Den was a horrible place, but Frank would have easily waded through a den of snakes to spend some time with Siena_the_Blade. *Would have* if she wasn't afraid of snakes, which she was. So she was relieved when they left the pool of hissing monsters and came across the redheaded Dice fighting a massive Cobra.

Of all the dungeons we had to choose, it had to be the one we *chose that had the player we were looking for.*

She could see why, although there were hundreds of different snakes in the dungeon, this was called the Cobra's Den. The boss's fangs were larger than the Ruby Edge Dice was using to fight it. However, it was obvious who Siena was honing in on, and Frank had to use her large body in an attempt to hold her back.

"We have to message Brock and get him to bring some back up!" she pleaded.

Siena shoved her arm down. "What are you talking about? I can take this carrot-top by myself."

"That's not the point, he'll just—"

"Whatever!" Siena jumped, using her massive shoulder as a fulcrum to flip over her and charge head first into the fight. "You call the others, but he'll be dead long before they get here!"

She was about to say that he would just run away, but was too busy messaging everyone to get a word out. She managed to annotate: "We located Dice, but Siena decided to rush in and fight him instead of calling for backup . . . " Then there was a flash and a swing from Siena's Reaper's Scythe that hit nothing but air.

Dice was gone and Frank decided to finish the message with: "He got away."

In her anger, Siena had finished off the Cobra with two quick slashes of her scythe and walked back to her with a sheepish grin on her face.

"Well, that didn't work out as I'd planned."

Frank nodded with wide eyes. "You think?"

"Don't worry, Efty! We'll get other chances!" She turned with a flourish, her scythe vanishing from her hands. "I have the item tracker after all!"

"Why do you keep calling me Efty?"

"Efty. F . . . T . . . FranktheTank! It makes a lot more sense than calling you *Frank*." Siena began moving back through the den. "Frank's a boy's name. At least Efty sounds a little more androgynous."

Frank sighed, not knowing how she should feel about such a nickname. "I guess I should be flattered."

Despite the nickname not sounding very flattering.

"That's the spirit!"

She followed her through the dark tunnels. Siena

equipped her scythe again and began cutting through the snakes slithering along the ground like she was mowing through grass, grass with fangs that hissed and bit you when you passed. Frank was just glad she didn't have to deal with them.

A message popped up in her notifications, and hoping it was a reply from one of the other teams, she brought it up. It was a message from Tessa.

She still hadn't talked to her since she had given her the instructions to meet with Dice, instructions that turned out to be a trap. After reading the message, however, she began to think she was either ignorant of who Dice was, or had more nerve than she gave her credit for.

Her message read: "Did the trade go well?"

Does she not know?

She found it suspicious that she was messaging right after Dice had been attacked by someone she had been seen with.

While she continued to follow Siena, she wrote back: "How well do you know Dice?"

Her reply appeared immediately: "Why? Was he rude?"

"You could say that. His team showed up and stole my orb, then killed me and took my armor."

Tessa's next message confused her even more: "But how? It was a Secotier dungeon! He had more than enough to buy it from you and still have Moola to spare! He showed me the numbers!"

The memory of being in the Broken Clock Tower hit Frank like a freight train. The person who had tricked her into giving away the orb was not Dice. It had been the one they called Data. It had all gone wrong after that. Maybe Dice had planned to buy the orb off her honestly and it went wrong after *they* showed up.

But no, they chased me before he took it! Were they trying to make me panic so I would give the orb to Data freely?

From Siena's response to his betrayal, it seemed she knew Data better than most. Frank decided to postpone her grudge until she knew more about what was going on.

She messaged Tessa: "I'll catch up with you later."

"I seriously didn't know anything!" was her last message before Frank put away the message window.

"Siena, what kind of person is Data?"

Siena shrugged. "I don't know. I thought I did, but now I'm not so sure. I thought he had a moral code he followed, but now he's either turned his back on that code, or he's a lot cleverer than any of us thought."

"What do you mean?"

She sighed. "I don't know! Ask someone else."

Frank nodded and decided she would. It seemed there was more going on between this little group of friends than she'd first thought. The night light shone down upon them as they exited the cave, coming to the Gateway that led out onto the Onjira Barrens.

Siena moved toward the Gateway. "Alright, let's meet back up with everyone."

And let them know how badly we screwed up.

Chapter 17
Hope

The Penance Mines were mostly the same as when I had first visited them. I moved into the cool shadows, hearing the clanging of chains and hammering of stone further down the shaft. The Gold Farmers were working as always, using earth magic to pull up big piles of dirt as their partners would begin sifting through it. Of course, this wasn't why I was here.

I picked up my pace along the soft soil as the wall torches began to light my way through the darkness into their depth. The last time I had done this Basetier dungeon, I had just started playing and was being shown the ropes by Data and Siena. Now I was a Wanted ranked player who could take down a party on my own.

Unless they can respawn right after they die, that is.

Up ahead I noticed a pair of boulders with wiry arms and grouchy faces. They were Rock Demons. Waddling over to each other, they would hoist their brothers above their heads and toss them at any passerby. I cast an Ice Coffin at them both and shattered them with the staff-end of my

Boomstick.

I took out the Rock Demons and Lantern Spirits, a new addition to these dungeons I hadn't seen before. The fires of the lantern hanging above us would float down and try to hit me, but like the flames they had emerged from, they were weak to my Water Hose spell. Once I had cleared my path of them, I could hear water dripping from the rocks and soon realized that it wasn't from my spell

As I had remembered, there was an inside waterfall that dropped through the gap in the cave's ceiling. As I approached the end of the dungeon where Siena and I had fought the Golem, I saw a figure sitting by himself between two puddles at the dead end. Having already defeated the Golem, Data was waiting for me by the rock pools.

"I'm glad you remembered." He nodded as though satisfied by this. "I think this was the second dungeon we did together."

"And I'm sure my parents paid you well for it. Why did you message me?" I asked, not wanting to waste time.

He shook his head, as though both amused and ashamed of himself. "I was so sure I was right, Noah. I was sure that Wona couldn't have covered up something like that . . . I wouldn't listen to you."

I suddenly realized what he was getting at. "You watched them, didn't you? The videos of the beta testers overdosing. You saw them before you handed it over!"

Data dropped his head in agreement.

"Then why?" I shouted. "Why did you give them the orb? That was the only copy, our only chance to make them pay for what they did!"

"Tsh, I didn't . . . it wasn't . . ."

He shook his head again and stood up. He held his hand up and a Transfer Orb appeared in his grasp, glowing in the dim light of the cave. My brow furrowed in confusion, but what he said suddenly made sense to me.

"You made a copy?" My eyes bulged as I looked down. "That's why Bitcon's team were still after Frank even after he'd had it stolen; they didn't know that you were the one who had it! That's why they didn't stop until you messaged them! Giving you just enough time to . . ."

He nodded and I couldn't stop the grin that spread across my face as he finished for me. "To watch the videos and copy them onto another item. I thought a Transfer Orb would be fitting, all else considering."

"And by handing over the original, you got to save face, leaving them ignorant of what you did." I laughed out loud, but my frustration quickly returned and I shouted, "Why did you wait so long to tell me?"

"I had to think about it." His voice remained solemn. "Noah, this is some heavy stuff. Having the evidence to take down the biggest gaming company in the world is not something to act rashly on. I feel that, after all you went through, you deserved to decide what would happen next."

Data handed me the orb and . . . I had it. The thing I was trying so hard retrieve was actually in my hands. Brock was going to freak out when he saw it.

That's right, Brock!

"I guess you and Brock don't have any reason to be angry with each other anymore?"

Data looked down. "Tsh, I was wrong. I'll have to apologize to him for that, but that'll need to wait. For now, I have to keep up the facade that I work for Wona. After what

I did, I've been offered a more technical job that will give me more power over what goes on in the game."

"So you can help us from the inside?"

He inclined his head and it suddenly made sense to me why he had spoken so vaguely about where to meet up in his message. It was so no one could track him and find out what he had done.

"Whatever comes next, I don't want to be anyone's scapegoat. I was asked if I wanted to join *Catastrophe* after what I did, but I couldn't . . ."

Catastrophe?

I held up the orb. "I understand. Either way, I'm thankful."

I turned to make my way to the Gateway.

"Don't rush into anything, Noah!" he called. "Think it through. Wona has more power than some developing nations! Once this gets out—"

"I get it, they're a werewolf!" I raised the orb up victoriously. "And this is my silver bullet. I have to make sure I hit the heart."

It didn't take me long to retrace my steps back through the mines. However, this time I took a left before the hollow where the farmers mined and headed down the shaft toward the Gateway. We were supposed to all meet back up outside Yarburn twenty minutes ago, and I hoped everyone was still around.

When I appeared on the beach and saw that they were all there and looking rather down, I smirked and swaggered my way over them. As I caught sight of Chloe, she avoided my eyes until I was right in front of her.

"We all failed to get anything out of our little team

excursion besides some Resource Items." She looked up as though trying to defy her obvious feelings for me. "What are you smiling about?"

I thought this would have been the best opportunity to tell them, but before I could, Brock stood from the bench.

"Speak for yourself." He pulled out a long piece of material. "I ran into Bitcon's Spellcaster after I searched Ice Castle, and look what he was wearing."

I suddenly recognized the garment in his hands. "Is that my Night Down Robes?"

Brock grinned, the first honest grin I'd seen on his face since we had returned from the Broken Clock Tower. He passed over the item and I equipped it. The robe flowed over my body and I gripped Brock's shoulder.

"You're a true friend," I said and patted him on the back. "But you're not the only one who found something on their mission."

Chloe raised her brow at me. "But we didn't find any—"

I put a hand up, not wanting her to give anything away before my big reveal.

"Voila!" I shouted and brought out the orb.

It shone in the warm light that bathed the Yarburn coast, giving emphasis to my discovery. Everyone fell silent.

Frank, who looked exhausted after his dungeon run with Siena, was the first to speak up. "Is that my Transfer Orb?"

I inclined my head to the Heavy. "It can be after we get the videos we need from it. The evidence on this orb should be enough to make Wona confess to what they did to Brock's friends. That's why we've been trying so hard to get our hands on it."

Frank's mouth made an 'o' shape, but then she frowned,

as though still puzzled by everything that was going on.

Brock's eyes dropped to the orb. "But how did you—?"

"I thought Bitcon destroyed it!" Keri exclaimed.

I shrugged. "Let's just say he wasn't thorough enough."

Siena bared her teeth in a smile. "Whoa, Noah! You little miracle maker!"

Brock shook his head in confusion. "Did you find a ghost file . . . or did you make a copy before you dropped it? No, you couldn't have . . ."

"Well, *I* didn't."

"Data . . ." Siena said, nodding in amusement. "I knew his betrayal wasn't all it was cracked up to be. Not him."

Keri screamed for joy and hugged Chloe. David laughed and whacked Frank on the back. Brock put a hand on my shoulder and grinned a familiar cheesy grin, looking like he was holding back tears.

We may not have gotten Siena's Ruby Edge back, but we had gained something much more valuable. The fact that a team made up of two Heavies, two Range, two Spellcasters, and including Data, two Warriors had outsmarted the creators of game itself seemed reason enough to celebrate.

Chapter 18
Rolling the Dice

Frank arranged to meet up with Tessa for a Primatier Dungeon on Jossi Island, a newer setting a few kilometers off from the Yarburn coast. She assumed this had come about out of the popularity of Yarburn itself, however, the inhabitant NPCs contained features more similar to Pacific Islanders than any other culture.

Flax and palm trees covered the island. She brushed some of the drooping fronds aside as she made her way off the beach and into the bush. There were no Gateways on the island and the canoe ride she had to take from Yarburn was supposed to be a fun way to explore the ins and outs of the archipelago on the way to Jossi. However, Frank hadn't had the time as she was already late for her meet up with Tessa.

But why meet on this island? Is it a trap or does she really just want me to try a new dungeon?

She was not sure whether or not she could trust her yet, but she was willing to give her another shot. The dungeon she had suggested going to was an underwater level that tanks were useful for, as they could sink to the bottom and collect all of the Resource Items on the ocean floor. First, they would have to find the ability that would allow them to breathe underwater.

She eventually found a path through the brush. It was a thin walking track that weaved between the trees. It led out to Nakoia Village where many of the NPCs were walking around, the women in long dresses, the men in singlets and shorts or lava-lava with nothing covering their muscular torsos.

Frank could see why Tessa wanted to meet here, and for someone who enjoyed looking at muscular men, she couldn't blame her, despite her apparent in-game identity. Finally, she found Tessa sitting on the edge of a small bridge that went over the stream which ran through the village. She swung her bare feet back and forth over the clear water.

She looked up as Frank walked over the bridge, her weight bowing the bridge even more. "There you are! I was beginning to think you weren't going to show up!"

"I didn't know there wasn't a Gateway leading here and it took a while to take the canoe."

And I wasn't sure if I wanted to come at all.

Tessa looked down at the stream. "I'm sorry about what happened. I had no idea Dice was going to gang up on you or that your orb would get stolen." She stood up and gave her the most charming smile. "Do you forgive me?"

Frank shrugged. "It doesn't matter. I managed to get it back anyway."

Tessa's smile crumbled and Frank's suspicion that she knew more than she was letting on grew.

"What? How?" She shook her head, as though trying to recover from a slip of the tongue. "I mean, didn't you say it was stolen?"

I nodded. "I thought so, too. Anyway, where do we get the breathing underwater ability? I'm keen to get some shell armor from the Resource Items in this dungeon we're going to."

Tessa's eyes shifted, but she nodded and began to walk through the village. "Okay, I've heard you have to go to Mermaid Lagoon at the center of the island to get it."

Frank followed her as they made their way out of the village and into the rainforest. Bird monsters shot over the trees and lizards hung about in the branches along with monkey monsters called Raboons, although, with their fangs and matted fur, they made even baboons look cute.

Tessa seemed more interested in another subject.

"So how did you manage to get it back?" she asked, trying to make the question sound nonchalant.

Frank shrugged again, going along with her devil-may-care attitude. "Got a bunch of friends together, split up to a bunch of Tertiatier dungeons and eventually one of us found the player who took it."

"And you defeated him?"

"I dunno how they got it. I wasn't in that team. All I know is that they managed to get my Transfer Orb back."

Tessa pulled out her crossbow and shot a Raboon swinging toward them before it could strike. "Should have asked me to come. I could have helped out, too."

Yeah, I bet, she thought as she took out her own Raboon with a swing of her Broadsword.

They came across the Mermaid Lagoon an hour later. It was something out of an exotic fantasy, not only because of the layout of the waterfall and pool, but there were mermaids relaxing on the rocks as though waiting for them. It was overshadowed by a cliff that seemed the perfect height for diving into the pool.

They moved through the flax and ferns toward it. The mermaids had long hair and their scales shimmered in the light that reflected from the pool. It made sense to Frank that an ability which allowed players to breathe underwater would come from creatures that could do just that. Coming to the edge of the lagoon, the mermaids jumped from their rocks and swam over to them, surfacing with adoring expressions.

"Would you ladies like to explore the depth of the lagoon with us?" the redheaded mermaid in the middle asked.

Frank caught Tessa's eyes, feeling their dialogue would be different if they were both men. *I really need some new armor!*

"Sure!" Tessa said.

Frank raised a brow at her. "Is this how—?"

"Shhh!" Tessa put a finger to her lips. "We would love to come explore the depth of the lagoon with you, but only if you allow us two the ability to breathe underwater, okay?"

The mermaids giggled and flipped back in the water like synchronized swimmers before lifting their hands from the water. A glow rose from their fingers and flew over to them. A window popped up saying.

— LEARNED ABILITY 'AQUA LUNGS' —

Tessa breathed out and grinned. "These mermaids are like sirens from *The Odyssey*. I thought there was something suspicious about the way they were acting."

Funny you should say that.

Frank turned from the lagoon and began to move back into the bush, hearing the mermaids calling an, "Aww" as Tessa followed after her.

When Tessa walked past, she gave Frank a puzzled look. "We've already spent an hour tramping through that forest. Why can't we just use your Transfer Orb to get back to the beach?"

Frank bit her lip. "You'd like that, wouldn't you?"

Tessa nodded as though this was obvious. "Well, yeah. I came here to breathe underwater and explore the sea, not go for a nature walk."

"That's not what I mean, you know—"

A large green lizard crawled down a tree branch behind Frank and its long, pointed tongue shot out at her. Catching it in her peripheral vision, she leapt back and cut it in half with her Broadsword. At the same time, Tessa shot at it with an arrow. The arrow ricocheted off her sword and went sailing through the trees.

Frank turned to her in the silence after the echoing *pang*. However, after seeing where she was standing, Frank's eyes bulged as understanding dawned on her. With how big she was, there was no way Tessa could have seen the lizard attacking. The arrow had been meant for her.

"Tessa . . . why?"

She reloaded her crossbow and aimed it again. "Who has it now?"

Frank looked around. "Are you trying to threaten me?"

She lowered her bow and sighed. "Can't you just tell me who has it?"

"What? So you can tell Dice, or whoever you were working with to steal it?"

Tessa ground her teeth and stomped the ground. "You don't get it! You don't know who these people are!"

"Wona's in-game hitmen, right?"

"You don't even know their name, do you?" Tessa said in exasperation. "They're *Catastrophe*, because that's all they bring to the people that cross them!"

"I don't care what they're called!" Frank growled. "You sold me out to them!"

Tessa shook her head in agitation. "They said they would pay you the Moola . . . but now . . ." Her voice broke. "If they know I led them wrong . . . Come on, Frank! Just tell me who has the orb!"

They must really want the evidence on there if they're hounding Tessa to get it.

"If you must know, it was a guy called Noah! But it doesn't matter anyway. He won't enter the Dream State now that he has the orb!"

Oh crap, why did I . . . ? Crap!

Frank paused, realizing what she had just done. Tessa nodded and then looked around quickly, as though afraid of her surroundings. She then turned and jumped, leaping from tree to tree to the edge of the forest.

"Tessa, wait!" Frank called, but she was already out of view.

She knew she couldn't catch her. A Heavy chasing down a Range Niche was a near impossibility. Nevertheless, she realized the implication of saying Noah's name. They would be on his tail if he stepped into the Dream State.

She brought up her messages and began to annotate: "Noah, they know you have the orb. Don't go back in the game!"

Chapter 19
Invitation

I'm not an idiot. At least I don't consider myself one. The first thing I did as soon as I returned to reality was make copies of the video files, a lot of copies. I used Brock's software to convert the Dream Engine files into regular digital video files and put them on as many devices as I had on me. I also made sure to remove the Transfer Orb from my inventory so no one could steal it before I could give it back to Frank. The evidence was finally safely within my grasp.

I should have emailed them to everyone I knew as well, but something in Data's words had warned me that I should be cautious with how they were delivered to the public. There was no going back once the genie was out of the bottle, and I wanted to make sure I wouldn't regret my wishes once I'd made them.

However, there was one person I felt deserved a copy of the video files as much as I did, someone I trusted emphatically. I messaged Brock to meet me in the Barrens north of Onjira after lunch to collect his copy, which I had encoded onto one of my Wakizashi. We both had mounts to get out there and I knew it was a place where no one would try to bother us.

Besides, with him still on the run after breaking me out and me lying low at David's apartment, I thought if I couldn't give it to him in person I could at least give it to him in-game. When I exited the Gateway and the smell of Onjira's poor district wafted over me, I regretted not just telling Brock to meet me somewhere else.

I strode through the bazaar. The market looked like something out of an ancient Arabian city, full of passing men and women smoking hashish pipes with curtains covering dusty store windows. As most of the faces of the NPCs were covered, you could easily tell who was a player by who didn't fit in among them.

That's why I found it strange that one of the male NPCs was following me. I noticed him out of the corner of my eye every time I turned a corner. He was a man wearing a headscarf and a long, red kaftan. I walked in a circle around the bazaar to be sure, but once I had failed to lose him, I made a beeline to the outskirts.

When I exited into the desert, I found a sign staked into the hardpan. On it were wooden boards carved into arrows that pointed in the direction of the rainforest, the desert, the barrens and the hills leading to the Druids' Keep Gateway. I turned to see if the man had been following me and jumped when I received a notification for a message.

FranktheTank: "Noah, they know you have the orb. Don't go back in the game!"

Oh, crap!

I went to leave . . . when an arrow hit me, pinning my robe to the signpost. I tried to pull free but I was stuck in place. I turned to see the man in the kaftan take aim and fire another arrow at me. It hit me in the thigh like a deep muscle injection, not taking away any Hit Points, but just paralyzing me.

The man then pulled off his head scarf to show a tangle of red hair beneath. It was the player Frank had called Dice, the Range who had worked for Bitcon's team and the one who had stolen Siena's Ruby Edge. He gave me a look of impatience and lowered his bow.

"I'd say that you shouldn't try to run," he said and looked up at the sun in the north. "But you won't be able to for at least half a minute anyway."

I stopped struggling, realizing its futility. "What do you want?"

He shrugged as though he wished he was somewhere else. "I'm just here to give you an invitation, and directions should you choose to accept it. I suggest you do, but that's just me."

"An invitation from who?"

"President Windsor Wona." He grinned when seeing my shocked expression. "Right? I was surprised myself. Who would have thought that one of the richest men IRL would care about a person like you? Not me."

I couldn't help but ask the next obvious question. "Why?"

"Something about a proposal." He shrugged again and stretched out his arm, passing me a piece of brown paper between two fingers. "Anyway, take this."

I looked at it skeptically, not knowing if I should take it or not. "What is it?"

"A map to the meeting place." He rolled his eyes when I wouldn't take it. "It's not going to bite. Look, once you take it, I can piss off, so just take it."

Curiosity more than anything made me take it. After I did, Dice turned, pulled out a black Summoning Stone and called forth his black dragon. I remembered how Brock and I had fought him on it above Sky Island while trying to escape Bitcon's team.

The giant wings rose and fell and he took off into the cloudless sky. I studied the paper and the item pulled up a full map of the Dream State in my vision. It included places I didn't even know existed in the game with a dotted line to one of the many places I hadn't explored north of New Calandor.

The map zoomed into the image of a place in the sky similar to Sky Island, but instead it looked like a city in the clouds. It was simply called 'Heaven'. At its northernmost point, and in fact the northernmost part of the map, was a lighthouse called Apollo's Lookout.

Above the map, it had a timer counting down the twenty-four hours I had to use it, stating:

— THIS MAP WILL BE INACTIVE IN: 23:42 —

As the clock continued its countdown, I wondered if I should go. At this point I had all the leverage I could need against them. They didn't know who I had given copies of the footage to, so I couldn't figure out what he could have possibly wanted to see me for.

Maybe he has an offer and wants to try and bargain with me. It might be amusing watching them try to buy my silence. Besides, I have an hour before I have to meet up with Brock, and if I talk to him in-game there's nothing he can do to physically threaten me.

I was most interested in meeting the person who had created the Dream Engine and orchestrated the ruining of my life. What kind of person could control an entire company and make back alley dealings with murderers on the side? It was both scary and fascinating, and as crazy as the idea was, I *was* interested in hearing what he had to offer.

I must be crazy, but I guess I'll know for sure when I can measure myself against a truly crazy person.

Chapter 20
Heaven's Gates

Just as New Calandor had been before doing a Tertiatier dungeon, there was no option to go to Heaven in the settings list. When I accessed the Gateway in the Onjira Village and saw this, I figured I would have to go there by riding Peragon from New Calandor, which I had been planning on doing anyway.

I selected New Calandor on the map and quickly made my way out of the city. I summoned Peragon and took off over the valleys and gorges that followed the harbor bay up the coast. The beautiful but ragged countryside reinforced the western frontier style setting along with canyons perfect for shootouts and a railway track that cut right through them. I wondered if this involved any 'Cowboys and Indians' dungeons but doubted it. The social implications alone would be enough to give Wona some bad PR.

I continued to fly over the gullies and stretches of fields that seemed to go on until the end of the map.

It's funny that I first thought the Storm Wall in the Barrens was the end of the Dream State. I wouldn't have guessed that it only splits the two eras between whether or not gunpowder and firearms can be used.

On the ocean's horizon I could see several naval ships that made up a battle fleet as well as a large island further north. I could only guess at the different dungeons and adventures these places contained, however, the dotted line on the map went straight over a small port town at the end of the land.

I shot down toward it, feeling the rush of warm wind that always impressed me with its attention to detail. I thought I would have to at least mention that when I met President Wona. My assumption of the port town was that it was an incomplete setting. This was not only because there were no ships in the harbor but because it was simply called 'Land's End'.

However, as I came closer I noticed large landing platforms that reached out over the ocean and gasped upon seeing what was on them and what it meant. The place had airships, like blimps with steam powered motors on either side of them. What Brock had said to me suddenly made sense.

So the third era he was talking about is distinguished by steam power and coal power. But it has archaic weapons and vehicles as well . . . so, does that mean it's a steampunk world?

The fashion of NPCs was similar to New Calandor, if a bit rougher and more conservative, keeping the corsets and suits, but removing the puffy dresses and white wigs. Although I was tempted to go down and take a look at the port or take a ride on an airship, I had been exploring for going on two hours now and didn't know how long it would take for me to get to the meeting place once I reached Heaven.

I soared upward over the water and continued ascending, looking for any sign of land. It seemed I really had reached the end of the map when I noticed a change in the color of the water. It went from a light blue in the sunlight to a darker blue in the shadow of what was above.

I gazed up and saw the massive clouds overhead. They took up most of the northern sky, and I couldn't help but think that above me was an entire setting dedicated to the theme that Land's End had only touched on. They looked like the clouds over the Penance Peaks, but instead of being gray and ominous, they were white and fluffy.

As expected of a place called "Heaven."

I pulled up on Peragon's shoulders and rode it up into the massive, blinding white of the clouds. The air was cooler now as I passed up through the mist, slowing Peragon down so I didn't run into anything up there.

When I emerged from them, the first thing I saw was a landing platform. Next to it was a sign saying: "NO STEEDS HEREAFTER." I was blocked by an invisible barrier as a window popped up telling me to dismount. I did so and dismissed Peragon, now able to walk through the barrier and look around in awe of the place. Think of heaven and then double it and you might have an idea of what I was seeing.

The giant clouds filled the horizon with only the barest hint of a city that I could just make out in the distance. The only thing that blocked me from going there was another giant barrier, this one visibly made up of huge golden gates.

If those airships I saw before are only used as Gateways like the ship to Pirate Cove and the horses to Ghost Town, this must be the barrier to the next era just as the Storm Wall is the barrier to the gunpowder era.

"This is nuts," I said as I approached the golden gates.

As I arrived, a window popped up on my screen that said: "Heaven's Gates: Restricted Access. Speak to Sentry Peter to gain access."

I looked up to see a large podium standing to the left side of the gates. Standing behind it was a bald man with a long beard, but instead of wearing flowing white robes like you would expect of a Saint Peter character, *Sentry* Peter was wearing a uniform like a guard of a superior station, complete with suit and bomber hat.

He seemed to see me and called, "Come forth, child."

His voice was booming and compelled me to move forward to take a closer look at the podium.

"What is your name?" he asked.

Wouldn't Saint Peter know my name? Or are they really just using the Heaven theme as an allegorical metaphor? Perhaps you can fight angels and demons in there.

"Noah Newbolt," I said.

The old man pulled out a large ledger and began looking through it. "Ah, Newbolt. Oh dear, you are guilty of very many sins."

I frowned. "Like what?"

He tapped the piece of paper. "While you have been in the game you have stolen, murdered, committed adultery, and most egregiously, disobeyed direct commands from our Lord Creator."

President Wona didn't create me. Still, I'm surprised he was paying so much attention to me while in-game. From the adultery thing, he must even know about Chloe kissing me while Sue was still alive.

"I have weighed your sins and found you wanting,"

Sentry Peter declared.

"So with these sins I can't get into Heaven?"

He closed the book with a thump. "There is no man without sin, Noah Newbolt. All you have to do is ask for the Lord's forgiveness and make amends for your transgressions. Only then will you be granted access to Heaven."

Yeah . . . right.

"How will I do that? Where do I meet him?"

"All you need to do is call on him and you will be in his presence." Sentry Peter spread his arms. "Ours is a kind and gracious Lord."

"Okay then," I said, and then in my most belligerent voice, said, "Hey Windsor! I'm here! Let's get this thing over with! I have lawyers that need talking to!"

Sentry Peter frowned, and at first I thought nothing would happen, but then a gap opened up in the pathway in front of me with a staircase leading down into darkness. At first I thought this was analogous to descending into hell, but as I looked up at the old sentry, he just gestured me forward.

"Our Lord awaits."

I nodded suspiciously and began down the stairs into the darkness. The staircase was long with red lighting that went down each wall, as though to prove my suspicions of its hellish theme. However, I had already done the Sulfur Pit and there wasn't anything fiery or brimstone-ish about the room I was approaching.

How could this be worse than that?

When I finally reached the end of the staircase, I saw that I was in a small dark room with two cushioned swivel chairs between a small table and a bright screen embedded into the back wall. It resembled a private movie theater, but much cozier.

I walked further in, feeling cautious, when I noticed that someone was sitting on the right-hand chair.

"Come and sit down, Noah. You have nothing to fear," a clear, commanding voice said.

I came to the chair on the left and sat down in it, looking at the blank screen. I turned to see the man sitting next to me. He was a handsome Asian-American man wearing a suit. He had an air of intelligence about him from the way he held himself. He smiled at me as though it were a professional courtesy.

"I'm Windsor Wona, the one responsible for this place."

Chapter 21
The Truth

"Don't you mean *Lord Creator*?" I asked incredulously.

"Ah yes, that banter you're famous for." Windsor nodded in amusement, he was a lot more jovial than I had assumed for someone of his station. "I thought you would find that entertaining."

"You talk as though you've created this place with me in mind."

Windsor inclined his head. "What you really mean is that I talk as though I know you. Granted, there's only so much you can learn about someone in a month, but I feel that I got the gist of your character."

"Like what?" I asked, ready to deny anything he said.

"That Sue was your life before she was taken, and that you would do anything to see the ones who took her from you brought to justice."

There was silence as I realized there was nothing about this statement that I could deny. It was all there, my intent, my reason for being here, everything.

Windsor gestured out a hand. "But I'm getting ahead of

myself. I invited you here to make a proposal after all."

I crossed my arms. "What makes you think I'll accept anything you have to offer me?"

Windsor shrugged. "I don't, but you did accept my invitation, which shows that you're at least a little curious of what it might be."

He's not exactly wrong.

"I'm willing to humor you for my own amusement."

Windsor slapped the arm of his chair playfully. "That's the ticket! But first let's start with a little movie, shall we? I think you'll find this one rather enlightening."

He grabbed a remote control from the table between us and pressed a button. The screen came to life just like one of the previews played in the Galrinth theater district.

The first thing to appear was a black screen with the title: Wona Laboratories 2056 under the red Wona logo, a red *W* made to look like a game controller. The video was set over four years ago.

"This isn't just the history of your company, is it?" I asked.

Windsor shook his head. "Oh no, this film was made just for you."

"Propaganda," I muttered.

The first video showed silent security footage of a group of young men and women standing around watching a demonstration of a vintage Dream Engine helmet. A man in a lab coat was putting it on and taking it off again. Although I couldn't read his lips, he must have told a joke for the whole group laughed.

"Notice anyone familiar in that crowd?"

It wasn't until he said this that I recognized a boy at the back of the crowd. Although he was younger, I could tell it was definitely Brock by his fair hair and cheesy grin.

"Your friend has been a part of this company in some way or another since its very conception," Windsor narrated as the screen went black again.

The title: Wona Interview Room 2057, appeared on the screen and another security video appeared. Once again it showed Brock, but this time he was sitting at a table talking to a man in a suit. The man passed him a slip of paper and Brock began filling it out. The camera zoomed in to show what it was. It was a job application.

At the bottom of the application, boxed in red was a non-disclosure agreement. The video played, showing as Brock came to the end and signed it before handing it back. The video then changed to a still photo of the application with 'Evidence 1' scrawled in red across it.

I'm beginning to see where this might be going.

The next video showed three clips cut together of Brock playing on a gaming station similar to an arcade style driving simulator. His hair length and clothes changed with each clip as the years 2057, 2058 and 2059 appeared in the corner of the screen.

"He enjoyed working for us. The fact that he stayed with us for three years should tell you that much." Windsor leaned forward and linked his hands in front of his face as the screen went blank again.

Another title appeared: Wona Laboratories 2059, soon followed by 'Evidence 2' Missing: File Corrupt.

A missing file?

"Unfortunately, we no longer possess working copies of these videos, but I don't think you need to see them again anyway. I'm sure you've seen them already."

Windsor eyed me, and I realized from his look that this was where the videos of the beta testers being overdosed was supposed to slot in.

A sudden confusion rushed over me. *Unfortunately? Wait, they actually want those videos as evidence? Then why did Bitcon crush the orb to delete them?*

The next title read: Wona Interview Room 2059. The video showed Brock looking much older than in the first video. He was once again sitting at a table opposite a man in a suit. He looked sleep deprived and distraught with gray rings under his eyes. Like in the second video, he was passed a piece of paper over the table, and although reluctant, he began to fill it in.

The camera once again zoomed in on the document showing the title: Confidentiality Agreement. My mouth dropped as I clearly saw on the video as Brock signed the agreement at the bottom. The video switched again to a still image of the confidentiality agreement and then a consent waiver, each with Brock's signature clearly scrawled at the bottom and the words 'Evidence 3' and 'Evidence 4' written in red across them.

So, they didn't forge his signature. Brock lied to me!

The screen went blank again and the next title read: Wona Database 2060.

Unlike the previous security footage, this was a video of a dark room. After a momentary edit to skip forward, it showed a young man walking between the computer desks, shining a penlight around the room. He sat down at one of the computers and booted it up before sticking a portable device into a USB slot.

From the light of the screen, Brock's features were clearly

visible. He went about using the computer, and although the screen wasn't facing the camera, what he'd told me he had done corroborated what the video was showing. The video paused on Brock's illuminated face with the title 'Evidence 5' written in the top right corner.

"A little breach of conduct here. Breaking and entering, breaking a nondisclosure agreement, breaking a confidentiality agreement, perjury. All criminal offenses." Windsor sighed. "Each of the beta testers knew the risks of the drugs we were testing on them. We can go back through all of the confidentiality agreements and consent waivers that were signed by them if you don't believe me."

"I see what you're doing." I ground my teeth. "It won't work on me. Your men killed Sue. That's all that matters to me."

"I thought as much." Windsor pointed to the screen. "But *this* is all that will hold up in court. Proof that your friend broke his agreements and broke the law. I don't know how long he could end up in jail for. We could always go easy on him, but . . ."

Is he really trying to blackmail me with this?

"I don't care!" I shouted. "You killed Sue!"

Windsor nodded, as though listening to me, but not agreeing. He pressed the play button. "This is where your involvement comes in, or should I say this is where Sue's involvement comes in?"

He flicked over Sue's old website with her petition to get the DSD banned from stores as well as the promise of evidence that would put Wona away. He fast-forwarded over most of her video blogs she had made pointing out how evil the Wona Company was.

"Really, there's no point in dredging all this up again. I'm sure you've heard these authoritarian arguments made a hundred times when you lived with her."

I gripped the edge of my seat in an attempt to control my anger. "What's your point?"

"The point is this." The videos changed into an interactive computer screen as Windsor used the remote to pull up an email inbox. He clicked on the search bar at the top.

Wait a minute . . . is he showing me his emails? Why would he show me his emails?

Windsor typed in "Sirswift" and a list of all the emails to and from his nephew rolled down the screen, showing that his email address also included the name he used in-game. Windsor then scrolled down to just before the date of the car crash that had paralyzed me and killed Sue.

"Any ghost file tracker on the Internet will be able to tell you that I haven't deleted a single one, and I swear that the authenticity of each email will hold up in court," he said and clicked on an email written a week before the date of the crash. It read:

> Dear Samuel,
>
> It has just come to my attention that there is a girl with a lot of followers who is creating a petition that may lead to the company losing a lot of money. I want you to convince her to stop. You may use company funds to try and bribe her, you can try to scare her, but do not use violence. I make myself crystal clear on this. I don't want anyone connected

to Wona to be convicted on assault charges. If they find out we're related, it will look bad for the family. The links to her website and her details are attached below.

Regards,

Windsor Wona

(Wona CEO)

That's . . . Wona didn't . . . I couldn't believe my eyes.

"Samuel was always a bit of a vicious dog, loyal, but quick to bite." He exited out of his emails to show one more video.

This one was the silent traffic footage from the top of a street pole, showing the highway traffic lights where my adventures in the Dream State truly began. The scene played out similarly but not the same to how I remembered it. My car was at the red light with nothing ahead of it. It showed the car behind me and the smallest glimpse of a young Asian man behind the wheel.

The lights turned green and my car went to turn off of the highway. It was most of the way off the road when the car slowed, as though it had nearly stalled. I knew already that this was where I had blacked out from being under the influence of DSD. However, there was still enough space to go around me.

The speeding truck that crashed into me, unsurprisingly, had no logo on it, but I assumed from the rough paint job that it was a company truck. As it approached, it ever so slightly turned into the side of my car, flipping it off the road.

"Whamo!" Windsor called in place of actual sound. "I tell you, I'm surprised you got out of that with just a little brain damage."

Watching the moment that my life was changed forever as President Wona confessed that it was his nephew who did it drove me into a fit a rage. "Why didn't you have this one deleted, huh? Why did this one slip through? It's almost like you're building evidence in a case against your own nephew!"

Windsor winked at me. "Astute as always, Noah. And last but definitely not least!"

He pressed a button on the control and a familiar voice arose from the walls around us. "Because I was the driver who followed you onto the highway, and the truck driver who crashed into your car was this guy here! You're in here because of us!"

It was Bitcon, his exact words from when he confronted me in Rubik's Castle. It suddenly dawned on me why I had been invited to this meeting in the first place.

"You're going to use your nephew to get Wona off the hook! Bitcon and his team are your company's scapegoat!"

"Come now, Noah," Windsor chided, shaking his head. "It's not a scapegoat if the person being punished for the crime is the one at fault."

"B-but he's your own family!" I cried but stopped myself, not believing my own words when realizing I was defending him, the one who had killed Sue.

Windsor's friendly expression changed, and he gave me a grave look as he brought back the video of the crash, pausing it a second after the moment of impact. "He's a murderer,

Noah. Even if he wasn't the one behind the wheel of the truck, and trust me, Colban will be convicted along with him, Samuel is a self-confessed accessory to Sue's death."

So if Samuel Wona is Bitcon, Colban must be the name of the barbarian-looking Heavy in Bitcon's team.

I shook my head, not believing my ears. "Why didn't you have them arrested as soon as you found out?"

Windsor grinned at me again. "I was waiting for you, Noah. I knew putting you at the head of this would be the only way to help you finally put Sue's memory to rest. That's why I invested thousands of dollars into a Dream Engine powerful enough to get you into the Dream State despite your injuries. That's why there were always security guards outside your door at the hospital and rehabilitation center; so no one could harm you while you recovered. Heck, I even allowed Data to tutor you at half the usual price that other players would've had to pay for someone of his caliber."

I shook my head, his voice seeming to reach out to my rational mind.

"Don't you see? I was trying to help you recover the whole time! I had no idea Samuel was still trying to get at you inside the game!"

"But you gave him the orders to steal the evidence!" I was breathing hard now, trying to find a hole in what he was saying. "You had me lured to a dungeon to kill me and used Sue to do it!"

Windsor shook his head. "It's true that I wanted the orb. I'm a completionist, Noah, like most gamers. I love for everything to be gathered into a nice little collection to show off, especially evidence. Why do you think I didn't just wipe out every Transfer Orb in the game? I could have, you know.

But no, instead I sent players like Dice to go out and search the orbs to see which of them contained the videos."

I gaped at this revelation. *It's true, he could have just deleted them all. Why didn't I think of that before?*

"Heck, I had already given orders for Samuel to stand down from his command so Dice could take over. It was his job to retrieve the evidence from you, but Samuel caught wind of this and made his own plans, hoping to silence you so he wouldn't get caught." Windsor raised his palms. "As loyal as he is, Dice lacks the charisma to be a good leader . . ." He grinned at me. "But that's where you come in!"

My head was buzzing with the implications of all this new information. If what he had said was true, not only were Wona themselves innocent of killing Sue, but they were offering to help me bring the ones that were responsible to justice.

Could it really have all been just a big misunderstanding?

Chapter 22
Making a Deal

I was still whirling with the consequences of my discoveries when Windsor made his offer.

"Once Sirswift is behind bars . . ." He said his in-game name, as though trying to distance himself from his nephew IRL. "He'll need to be replaced. You've proven yourself to be a man who can lead people. The amount of times your friends have followed you into dungeons with near impossible odds shows you to be a charismatic leader."

I shook my head at the proposition. "You . . . want me to work for Wona?"

He nodded and spread his hands. "Catastrophe's new leader: Noah Newbolt."

Catastrophe . . . that's the group they wanted Data to join. Maybe we could . . . No! This is ridiculous!

"It's not so ridiculous, is it?" Windsor shrugged, as though he *could* read my mind. "Think about it this way. You can't trust I'll do what I say I will with my nephew."

"Damn right," I agreed.

"But you also know that I want you working for me.

If you work for me, you'll be able to witness every stage of Samuel's downfall from beginning to end with a front row seat." He lifted his eyebrows at me. "I'll put it in the contract."

"And I know how seriously you follow those." I couldn't seem to make this remark sound sarcastic after what he had just shown me.

Windsor raised his palms, as though it were obvious. "I'm a businessman."

"What about Brock breaking his agreement, then?"

If I have as much leverage as he says I do, maybe I can get a bit more out of this than just a job.

Windsor nodded, his eyes catching the screen again. "Well, the confidentiality agreement says he'll not share the information with anyone outside of the company. The way I see it, if you're a part of the company, he wouldn't have broken his contract, now would he?"

Wraps everything up with a nice little bow. I would almost consider it clever if it wasn't so cruel.

"But if you have a reason to trust me, I'll need a reason to trust you." He sighed. "Although the company won't be found guilty in any court for the beta-testers overdosing, the good name of the Wona Company itself is still at stake. If those videos become public, it will be a PR disaster and Brock will be charged with releasing private information. Do you catch my drift?"

I nodded. "So the deal is, I work for you in return for putting your nephew in prison, and for the videos, you'll leave Brock alone and clear him of all charges?"

"You have my word," he confirmed. "So long as no one else sees the videos, the contract will not have been broken, so there will be nothing to charge him with. So long as we work together, it will be mutually beneficial. You want to see Sue's murderers brought in front of a judge, don't you? It's a win-win."

I nodded, too deep in thought to agree to the deal right away. I wanted it, more than anything, but I wasn't willing to sign my name to anything just yet, not until I had all the information I needed.

"I need to think about it."

Windsor leaned back in his chair and spread his hands. "By all means, take as much time as you need. But remember, if the videos become public, this offer will become void. Think of it as a package deal."

I stood and went to make my way back up to Heaven's Gate, stopping before I reached the stairs. "I guess I can't get into Heaven until I sign on with you either?

He smiled and bowed his head. "Heaven is still in its testing stages. At this point it's only accessible by Hero rank administrators and Wona employees."

"Trying to sweeten the deal?" I asked.

He frowned. "I understand how you might see it that way, but that's just the rules for new dungeons. If you want, you can think of it as one of the perks of the job."

"I will." I turned and climbed the stairway to Heaven.

When I came out of the darkness, the bright light over the clouds was almost blinding. I squinted and saw Sentry Peter still at his podium. He raised his wrinkled brow at me, as though asking me if I wanted something. I turned, ignoring him in favor of leaving. I had enough on my plate after coming here.

Wait? Why did I enter the Dream State again?

I suddenly remembered that I was supposed to meet with Brock and pulled up my messages to see two notifications from him. The newest read:

Brockodile: "Where are you? I've been waiting in this rain for two hours!"

Crap!

I replied: "Where are you now?"

Brockodile: "Entry to the Barren's Rift dungeon."

I was about to ask where it was in the Barrens, but then remembered I still had time to use the map Dice had given me and decided not to bother.

"I'll be there soon."

Brockodile: "You'd better be. I'm soaked through!"

Instead of flying all the way to the Barrens, I summoned Peragon and flew down into the Land's End port town. Inside, it definitely hinted at the steampunk society beyond Heaven's Gates. I didn't get a chance to appreciate the clean, cobblestoned town before I landed at the Gateway to an airship landing pad.

As I'd thought, the Gateway was in the middle of the airstrip. I selected the Onjira Village, ran out of the city, and again called forth Peragon from my Summoning Stone. Flying through the mountains, it took me less than half an hour to get to the stormy wastelands of the Barrens.

I pulled up the map and found that the Gateway to Barren's Rift was just south of the Storm Wall. The sketches around the Gateway made it look like a massive crater in the already pockmarked land. The earth surrounding it was cracked with thick ravines, as though whatever lightning bolt had caused the hollow was involved with the story of the land itself.

I swooped down toward it, my robes becoming sodden in the rain. The water pooled at the base of the crater where the Gateway floated, and I was starting to think the rain wasn't the only reason Brock had become drenched.

I spotted him, a cloaked form on the edge of the crater's slope. He waved at me and I shot down toward him and jumped off my mount. I didn't plan on hanging around in the rain so I kept Peragon out. I was fascinated at the little character animation as my Pegasus-dragon hybrid began playing in the puddles, as though it felt at home in such a place.

"Hey!" Brock called. "Did you bring my copy of the videos?"

Oh, that's right! How to explain this without . . . wait a minute, he's my friend and he lied to me. Why am I the one walking on eggshells around him?

"Why did you lie about Wona forging your signature?"

I think this was my first question because talking to President Wona had agitated me. I was mostly agitated at myself for not being more suspicious of how Brock claimed to know about the forgery, despite the fact that no one had used the confidentiality agreement against him yet.

Brock's eyes widened but he played dumb. "Sorry?"

"Did you see the confidentiality agreement after you refused to sign it?"

"No." His brow furrowed, as though already aware of what I was accusing him of. "Why are you asking me this now?"

"It's just odd that you can so confidently say they forged your signature if you never saw it afterward." Despite this hole in his story, I decided I should give him an out. "It's almost like you're trying to cover up for a mistake you made."

Brock stepped forward. "What kind of mistake?"

I realized he wasn't going to admit it unless I spelled it out. "Oh . . . I don't know. That you signed it in distress and regretted it later, and so you lied about it?"

Brock's eyes hardened. "Who have you been talking to? Did Data—?"

"Why are you always blaming Data?" I stopped and shook my head. "I can't believe you would lie to me like that!"

Brock looked down, eyelids tightly closed. "Okay, fine! But it wasn't completely a lie, okay? When I signed it, I wasn't in my right mind. I was coming off of the aftereffects of whatever drugs I had been on at the time. The way they forced it on me when they did, they may as well have forged it themselves!"

This made sense, but I wasn't going to let it slide just like that. Windsor's words still weighed heavily on my mind.

"What are you going to do if I give you the videos?" I asked.

"Isn't it obvious?" He flicked his hand out, rain splattering from his cloak. "Make it public, show everyone with eyes to see it, and make Wona confess to what they did! What Sue always wanted!"

As soon as he tried to use Sue to make my emotions overtake my reason, I knew I couldn't give him the videos, no matter what he said.

"If you did, they would be after you." I then shouted, "You'd be guilty of everything they're accusing you of!"

"How would you know what they're accusing me of?" Brock looked at me in confusion, but then sudden understanding came over his expression. "You were approached by them, weren't you? They tried making a deal with you!"

I nodded. "I won't deny it. That's how I know you lied about them forging the agreement. That's how I know that you'll get screwed if those videos ever go public and they take you to court. They have everything recorded from when you first arrived at Wona Laboratories to the security footage of you stealing the videos!"

Brock raised his arms in exasperation. "Of course they do! Don't you think I know that? I've been on the run for the better part of a year! And now that I finally have the chance to clear my conscience, you're telling me that doing so will land me in even more hot water? I'm already too far in to pull out now, Noah!"

"There's a way out of it," I said.

Brock nodded dramatically. "And here it comes! Go on, tell me their offer! Does it happen to involve giving them the evidence and hoping for the best?"

"Listen to me. I'm the only one who you showed the videos to, right? Well, the agreement states that you can't show people outside the company, so if I join the company you wouldn't have t—"

Brock seemed to crack when hearing this. "Are you absolutely nuts? *Join* Wona? They killed Sue, for Pete's sake, Noah! Can you think of a better way of spitting on her memory than joining the very company that killed her?"

"It wasn't them," I said, although even coming from my lips, it sounded like a weak excuse.

"I must be going crazy." Brock palmed his forehead. "You told me, only a month ago, that Bitcon admitted to purposefully crashing a truck into your car! How is that not Wona's fault?"

"Bitcon didn't do that at Wona's request; his team did that on their own!"

"Oh, well, isn't that convenient?"

I could tell Brock had been pushed to his limits, finally having what he had been working for within arm's reach and realizing he wasn't going to get it. I knew what he must have been feeling, but I still had to try and get through to him.

"I saw the instructions they gave him. His team was only supposed to scare us," I said, not believing that I was defending Wona to my best friend.

"Of course!" Brock shouted sarcastically.

"Just listen to me, okay?" I tried to calm my head. "They're going to turn him in, they were planning on doing it from the beginning, but they wanted me involved."

Brock waved his hand in the air again. "A scapegoat, brilliant!"

"He's the one who killed Sue!" I then yelled, "I need this game, Brock!"

There was a crash of lightning then. During the flash and in the silence after it, I saw his face. I mean, really saw it, and in that instant, I knew why this was going to turn out badly for our friendship. From the change in his expression, I think he understood then as well.

"That's all that matters to you, isn't it?" Brock sounded like a broken man. "Staying in the Dream State . . . avenging Sue. So long as they put Bitcon and his men behind bars and keep you in the game, you couldn't give a crap about my friends who died."

I felt a deep ache pull in my chest as the full weight of

our disagreement hit me all at once.

I said, "Your friends made their decision as soon as they signed up to be beta testers."

With a flash, Brock's bow appeared in his hands and he was nocking an arrow and firing at me. On instinct, I leapt back to dodge it and cast an Ice Wall in front of me to block the second arrow he tried to shoot my way.

"What the heck are you doing?" I cried.

"I'm going to get that evidence!" Brock growled. "Even if I have to paralyze you, drag you to Tertiatier and loot it off your corpse!"

Chapter 23
Frenemies

Behind my wall of ice, I called Peragon over to mount it before Brock could run around and fire at my flanks. I took off, only barely dodging one of Brock's arrows as it whizzed past me. The wind and rain whipped at me as I flew. However, as I looked back, I saw that Brock wasn't going to give up so easily.

He had summoned his Ice Dragon, and, having the larger of the two mounts, he was quickly gaining on me. Afraid he might try to freeze me with his mount's Ice Breath, I tried some evasive maneuvers. However, this more or less had me flying blindly into the rain as he rushed to catch up.

An arrow zoomed past and exploded into a Fire Ball spell in front of me. I turned north to avoid it. In a sense, Brock and I had similar abilities. With my Boomstick, I could launch spells at greater distances, and with his specialty arrows, Brock could cast a spell at me with each one he loosed.

However, his arrows were limited to level two spells, while I had two level threes in my arsenal, and one of them was a spell that I didn't think his mount would like.

Or Brock for that matter, but he's left me no choice.

I cast a Cyclone spell behind me to catch up any arrows he might shoot, and then I spun to meet him. I gasped when I saw he was right on top of me, his dragon ready to launch its Ice Breath, which was as strong as a level three spell and more than enough to get through my Cyclone and freeze me solid.

I didn't hesitate. Raising my Boomstick I called forth my Wildfire. Fire and Ice met inside the cyclone in a tangle of hot and cold air. It blasted us away from each other. Mounts may not have Hit Points, but when we fell, they fell. Luckily we were far from finished and I pulled up . . . and hit the Storm Wall.

I suddenly realized why Brock had been constantly firing at my left side. He was trying to back me into the Storm Wall. It buffeted me, and bolts of lightning struck down to prevent me from going any further. I reared up and turned, racing down its edge.

Brock was hot on my tail, literally, after my fire spell. However, I also knew that he could only use Ice Breath once during a battle as it consumed all his Mana, and his one opportunity to freeze me had been canceled out by my most powerful attack. However, after casting Wildfire I was almost out of Mana myself, which meant I couldn't sling spells at him willy-nilly.

Once he caught up, I pulled away from the Storm Wall and we circled each other. Catching Brock's expression, I saw him looking pained but determined to catch me. I, on the other hand, would have left if given the chance.

If only I'd brought the Transfer Orb with me!

I ducked a few arrows, casting pathetic level one spells at him that did nothing but get in his way. We chased each other's tails, sometimes slamming into the Storm Wall in our attempt to dodge another one. The rain pelted down as the battle wore on, and although I knew I was losing, I faced him. I wasn't fast enough to flee from him after all.

"I know you have it on you!" Brock called as he caught up to me again. "I'll steal every item in your inventory if I have to!"

"Just think for one second, Brock!" I called back. "This will avenge Sue and make it so you don't have be on the run anymore! I'm doing this for both of us, don't you see that?"

"And let Wona get away with what they did to my friends?" Brock shook his head. "Never!"

"You can't prevent that!"

Brock sneered. "You're a coward."

This brought up the memory of Chloe's words to me after I called her a pessimist while being surrounded in the Broken Clock Tower. "The word you're looking for is realist!"

I was desperate enough to start pretending to give up, in the hopes of hitting him with a sneak attack, when a window popped up in my vision, distracting me. At the same time, Brock dipped his huge Ice Dragon's wings and slammed me into the Storm Wall. Peragon flipped backwards and spread its wings to steady itself. My Hit Points were dwindling from the attack, with less than a fifth left.

That's when I read what was in the pop-up window.

— PERAGON HAS LEARNED 'STORM HORN' —

I gaped. My mount had finally learned its attack, and

at the most perfect time. Yet I could only use it once, and considering I had never used it before, I didn't know what to expect.

I have to make sure it hits him!

I realized then that the only way to corner Brock was to use the Storm Wall. Peragon flapped its wings and I arced away from the wall, knowing the move would be my last chance to get away from him.

Brock aimed at me with an arrow, his back to the barrier of wind and lightning. I lifted my Boomstick and used the last of my Mana to cast one last Cyclone spell at him. The wind stopped the arrow, and as I had hoped, slammed him back into the Storm Wall, trapping him between the two winds.

I found 'Storm Horn' in my Key Triggers and activated it. Peragon's wings suddenly splayed and its body stiffened. Its lion legs shot out as though to support itself in the air. A pool of electrified energy began to rise out of its forehead, as though to form a horn like that of a unicorn.

A fork of lightning hit the tip of the horn, although I had no idea if this was a part of the attack or just the weather. The energy continued to build until it shone a bright white. It then shot forth in a beam of light, striking Brock and driving him deeper and deeper into the Storm Wall. Electricity flared all around him and a look of pain went through his expression.

Brock's Hit Points must have taken a beating during our fight as well, for after only a second, his avatar and the Ice Dragon were both obliterated against the Storm Wall.

I had won.

I don't believe it. He had Wanted ranks in Tertiatier, and I managed to beat him!

I couldn't help but grin at my success as lightning forked down around me. I then felt my face go grim as I realized what this now meant.

Brock, one of my best friends, was now my enemy.

Chapter 24
The Dragons' Nest

It made sense to Frank that this place, of all places in the Dream State, was Siena's favorite dungeon. The amount of levels in the canyon north of Toena allowed the redheaded Warrior a great deal of free space to move from ledge to ledge along the cliffs. Frank, on the other hand, had to edge around each of the dragon nests.

The way the dungeon worked was simple. Touch an egg and its mother will come, that mother being a fire-breathing dragon. However, the color of the egg determined the dragon, so to get the armor she wanted without being swarmed by hundreds of dragons, she had to make sure only to touch the red eggs.

Frank thought she should feel lucky that a player like Siena_the_Blade would invite her to do another Tertiatier dungeon. However, she was beginning to think that maybe she should have earned her way here without having a partner who had accumulated far more Skill Points than she had. Frank would have waited until she had made up with Tessa, but Siena had promised her the special Dragon Armor a player could get there.

She either feels really bad about me losing my identity, or this really is her favorite place here.

She clutched the vines hanging down from trees at the top of the gorge to keep her balance. The ledges around the nest were narrow, making it hard for her to navigate her way through. Ahead of her, Siena was taking care of a Red Dragon on her own, having gone ahead and touched a red egg.

This is a Tertiatier dungeon. If we die here, I could lose all of my . . .

She paused in thought as she realized that after having a full set of armor stolen from her in the Broken Clock Tower, she had nothing left to lose. She grinned and stopped being afraid of falling. Using her strength to jump from ledge to ledge along the narrow cracks in the earth, she charged in swinging her Broadsword at the Red Dragon.

A giant claw hit her and knocked her against the canyon wall. She groaned, realizing that having lightweight stats definitely had a downside. Despite this, Siena grinned at her as she picked herself up.

"Now we're talking!" She raised her scythe and swung it at the dragon's snapping head, its fangs gnashing at her. "Come on!"

Frank charged in again, and with Siena distracting it, managed to get a few good slashes in before Siena finally cut the thing's head off. She breathed out and couldn't help but grin when seeing the fierce look on Siena's face.

"That's two," Siena announced proudly. "Just two more to go."

"Wait . . ." Frank frowned. "When did you get the first one?"

Siena shrugged. "I think it was when you were struggling to climb up those vines earlier. Don't get me wrong, you climbed faster than most Heavies I've taken here."

Frank's eyes narrowed. "Thanks, I guess."

Siena tossed her the red, steel-like dragon scale, the Resource Item they were trying to collect to synth her new armor. They were pretty large and she was surprised that four of them were needed to make the armor. Although, thanks to Siena, she doubted it would take too long to get them all.

— ACQUIRED 'RED DRAGON SCALE' —

They moved on and Siena exhaled, as though enjoying the illusion of fresh air.

"I really love this place. Not just because of the dragons but thanks to the shadows it's the coolest place in Onjira." She turned a grin Frank's way and she nodded. "And what better way to stay longer in a place like this than fighting with a newbie like you to help slow me down, eh Efty?"

Frank raised an eyebrow at her. "Flattering."

"Not really." Siena flicked back her ponytail and turned. "Playing with you is like driving a car with a failing battery."

Frank continued to follow her through the gorge, avoiding the black and blue eggs but taking the yellow eggs, for they gave Siena a temporary strength boost.

"Do we really need only four scales?" Frank asked.

"If you want a full set of armor, then yes." She flicked her head around, ponytail waving like a flag. "Isn't it great, you get to spend an hour with me!"

Frank nodded, bemused, but not entirely sure if she was grateful. Ever since she and Tessa hadn't been on speaking terms, she had also done a Secotier dungeon with David, Chloe, and Keri's group. It was a fun, Spanish, carnival-themed dungeon west of Galrinth, and Frank had enjoyed the banter between them while fighting the face-painted, voodoo-possessed zombies. She hoped they could do it again soon.

Maybe I should have asked Chloe and Keri to come with us on this one. Chloe in particular would have been really helpful to explore the different levels of this place.

The next red egg was found among a group of minor monsters. Several young dragons guarded it. Although they looked innocent enough, the flame they breathed at them when they drew near proved otherwise. Siena lost some Hit Points in order to cut through them with her Reaper's Scythe.

Frank had noticed that the mother dragons would only attack the player that touched their egg. Something about this put her on edge, but she couldn't figure out why. Even so, the feeling made her equip a magic defense shield she had won in a mining dungeon with Tessa before even meeting Siena.

It wasn't until they tried to get the third scale that she realized what the feeling was trying to warn her of. As soon as Siena crouched down to touch it, not only did a Red Dragon appear but several Range players from another party dropped from the lip of rock above them. They swung down on the thick vines and began to fire projectiles at them.

The dragon only attacks the player who touches their egg,

making them a perfect target for players to ambush them!

Seeing how many Hit Points Siena had lost from the Dragonflame, Frank knew that taking on both the Red Dragon and these players would be too much, even for her. Siena had underestimated the dungeons she was doing ever since she'd lost her Ruby Edge, and Frank knew now what this meant for ambushes.

"Look out!" she called.

Without hesitating, Frank jumped out in front of her, using her shield to block the oncoming arrows and throwing knives. She turned to see Siena spin about, the Red Dragon landing behind her.

However, the expression Siena made when she turned to see the other players was more in line with adoration than horror, as though they had just made her day.

"Oh, you guys . . ." she said, like they had just revealed a surprise party in her honor. "You really shouldn't have."

Instead of fighting the dragon, when its long neck swooped down to bite at her, Siena jumped up onto its head. Its head rose quickly, carrying her up the cliff face as though it were a lift. She flipped backward onto the ledge the other party had just jumped from and began using her scythe to cut the vines each of them were hanging from one by one.

One Range Niche yelped as he fell, another screaming until all Frank could hear were the running footfalls of the rest of the members in their party fleeing above her. Frank could have sworn she heard one of them scream, "It's Siena_the_Blade!" as he ran from her. Although she didn't see all of it, Frank was pulled out of her awe when the giant dragon reared up and shot Dragonflame at her.

She raised her shield to block the attack but the flames

didn't last long. Peering out from behind the shield, her mouth dropped when seeing Siena on top of the dragon's neck, her scythe's blade stabbing through its head and pinning the dragon's mouth shut against the ground. She grinned mischievously before pulling her scythe free and cutting off its head.

I'm beginning to think I underestimated her a little.

"Wow. You really do know this dungeon like the back of your hand."

Siena shrugged. "Well, I did say it was my favorite."

Frank nodded and decided to stop doubting her. She was well-known in the Dream State for a reason. She brought out her Broadsword and moved to follow Siena to the final red egg.

"Do you, like, not have any friends in the Dream State?" Siena asked, blunt as always.

Frank sighed. "I had one, and I usually played with her party."

"I'm guessing that she was the one who sold you out?" Siena raised an eyebrow. "Considering you're not playing with them anymore."

Frank nodded. "But I think there's more to it than just simple betrayal. She seemed scared the last time I tried to bring it up."

Siena nodded. "Catastrophe is a scary bunch. They work for Wona and aren't afraid of threatening people outside the game if things don't go their way. You should talk to Noah about them. He's suffered more from their actions than anyone else."

I might just do that. Maybe he can help me get Tessa out from under their thumb.

They found the fourth red egg on the ledge near the end of the canyon. Much to Siena's chagrin, Frank made sure to check the area before she touched it, making sure there was not another party around that could ambush them.

There wasn't, and like the previous three, they took the dragon down without much effort. Although after having used the yellow eggs to increase her strength, Siena didn't *need* any help. After it had vanished, Frank had everything she needed to make a full set of Dragon Armor.

Siena beamed. "You'll be able to go to New Calandor now as well."

Frank nodded, relieved that she wouldn't have to restrict her teammates to playing behind the Storm Wall. They weren't a bad group of people, and though she didn't always get along the best with Siena, she found herself getting used to her endearing, devil-may-care attitude.

It doesn't make losing Tessa any less painful, though.

Siena was suddenly looking out into space with bulging eyes, as though she had received a message from someone and was shocked by what it read.

"What is it?" Frank asked.

Siena turned to her, expression shifting from shock to horror. "Noah, he's . . . he's not going to do anything with the evidence."

Chapter 25
Obligations

My decision had already been made. Having evidence against Brock just lying around David's apartment in multiple devices was too risky. Skinny arms shaking from the effort, I quickly went about destroying them, almost breaking David's microwave in the process. I knew how easy it was to recover ghost files from a device with the right software, and couldn't risk someone else getting their hands on the evidence.

Brock was insistent on avenging his friends by taking on Wona. However, considering he wouldn't have a chance in court after signing the confidentiality agreement, I knew keeping the evidence from Brock was the only way to save him from himself.

The only copies I didn't delete were on the USB I decided to always keep on me and the one I had encoded into my Wakizashi, which I had to deliver to Wona upon signing the contract. I had to be careful. If one of them went astray, my deal with Wona and everything that came with it would be forfeit. Perhaps this even included the part about them putting Samuel and Colban in prison.

Now that I had accessed the Gateway at the airship platform at Land's End it was in the list of settings I could pick from when selecting areas on the map. I appeared on the high-rise landing after leaving Galrinth, hoping Brock had told no one about what had occurred between me and him.

From how he tried to use Sue's memory, I wouldn't be surprised if he tried using my friends against me as well.

I looked up in awe as one of the massive airships took off from a runway next to the platform I was on. Seeing the way the sun glistened off of its balloons and propellers as it ascended into the sky made me realize that I had been fooling myself all this time. The reason I kept returning to the Dream State despite what had happened to me wasn't because I needed to. I loved it here.

The beauty of the world, the excitement of the game, the escape from painful reality—particularly now that I was debilitated—all of these elements were brought together to create an experience that I had not only become fond of, but was partial to. I could now see why people became addicted to this game like David was, and now I was going to be paid to play it.

Instead of flying up to Heaven's Gates on Peragon, I decided that this time I would take an airship. As one landed and I was about to get on, I received a message notification from Siena. I ignored it, knowing exactly what it would be about. Especially since she would have heard everything from Brock's perspective, I could understand how my sudden change of heart would seem a little suspicious.

An NPC waved me onto the airship as it was taking off

and I walked up the ramp and made my way onto an open deck. I watched in amazement as the propellers began to spin, lifting me up into the air with the other administrators going to Heaven. In the distance, I could see players trying to catch a peek of what was going on inside the gates.

Our speed increased as we made our way over the ocean and up into the clouds. I went inside to have a look, but all that was in there was an unfurnished hall with, I was pleasantly surprised to the see, a viewing window in the floor. Although it currently showed the ocean hundreds of feet below, I could only imagine what it would be like to have the opportunity to ride one of these over the rest of New Calandor.

Message notifications popped up in my vision several times during my trip to Heaven's Gate and I ignored them all. If any of them were from Wona I would be speaking to their president soon, anyway. If they were from my friends, I thought it would be better to get this over and done with than drag it out.

I know what I'm doing.

At least I thought I did, and nothing at this stage was going to change my mind. Not when knowing that everything I had worked so hard on was now achievable. Bringing justice to Sue's killers, making sure my friends were no longer harassed, it was all within my grasp. Brock was just going to have to accept that his friends signed their agreements and no wishful thinking was going to turn back time and make it otherwise.

When the airship finally landed on the massive platform, I saw President Wona was waiting for me. He stood tall in front of Heaven's Gates, his Asian-American face set in a smile that was knowing and welcoming.

"Come, let's talk business."

The path we were walking down parted again and we descended down the dark staircase, leading to the mini-theater room where I had seen the security footage and evidence collection. However, instead of the small screening room, the room Windsor led me to was an interview room, an exact replica of the one that had been in the security footage. However, instead of man in a suit passing me across the form, it was Windsor himself.

"I will go through it with you just in case you don't understand some of the terminology." He pointed to the first line. "For later reference, in this contract you will be considered the employee and Wona the employer." His finger slid down the paper to a list of bullet points. "We must agree to do each of these within one month of signing this contract."

It read: The employer has agreed to:

> -Ensure the arrest of Samuel Wona and Colban Bay and provide all available evidence against them in court.
>
> -Drop all charges against ex-employee Brock Driver (on the condition that all evidence taken by him is returned to Wona).
>
> -Give employee Noah Newbolt the authority to control his own team under Wona, allowing him all the powers this consists of and an opportunity to employ and lay off team members until they are up

to seven in number.

The next section was everything I agreed to do within the month of signing the contract.

It read: The employee has agreed to:

> -Relinquish all copies of evidence from the information that was stolen by ex-employee Brock Driver.
>
> -Fulfill all obligations of a player under the Wona Company's employ, including but not limited to: Keep a functioning team of up to seven members, following company commands to a reasonable level, and demonstrate player skill.

"What does it mean by demonstrate player skill?" I asked, feeling my credibility and the fact that I had survived in here for a month demonstrated this already.

"Just a formality each player must go through before they are raised to the rank of *Hero*." Windsor made sure to emphasize the last word.

Hero rank . . . just like Data.

"What will I have to do?"

He smiled. "Complete a new dungeon in Heaven."

I had only heard of one dungeon in Heaven that had been completed and decided to make a guess. "Apollo's Lockout?"

Windsor nodded. "And by *complete* we don't mean just make it to the end. You have to kill every monster in the dungeon and . . . you'll need to put the evidence at its top to complete it."

"Why?" Noah frowned. "I could just give it to you now."

Windsor shook his head, as though amused. "What will that show? That you are willing to make a trade? That's not good enough, Noah. You need to show me you're willing to do what Wona desires. We need to test your loyalty before we can trust you."

I don't get it. Does Wona really have that much leverage over Brock that they don't even care if I give them these videos?

"Are you not willing to meet these obligations?"

"No!" I said, too quickly. "I'm willing."

Windsor smiled again. "Very good then. For now, this is a conditional contract. Once you've fulfilled the necessary obligations, it will be considered official."

He handed me a pen. After reading up on some of the terminology in the contract, I eventually signed it.

I'm doing this for my friends.

"Very good. Now that you are an employee with us you may enter Heaven and make your way through to Apollo's Lookout. I'd also recommend going through the stores and getting the best equipment you can find for your Niche. Heaven has some of the best gear in the Dream State."

I grinned. "I wouldn't have enough money for all that."

"Don't be so sure," he said, gesturing to me. "Check your Moola counter in your menu."

I did and gasped. There was no number for my amount of Moola, only a red infinity sign.

"You're joking."

Windsor shook his head again in amusement.

"I have unlimited funds?" I asked.

"And you'll also have every ability possible for a Spellcaster unlocked." Windsor almost laughed and I could tell the expression I was making made the excitement I felt as transparent as a pool of glass. "Only seems fitting for the leader of Catastrophe, right?"

I nodded. "Only if I put them to use."

I turned and moved up the stairs from the interview room, I felt lighter, as though my weight stat had gone down. In reality I knew that it was because the burden of being hunted by Wona had been lifted from my shoulders. Bitcon and his teammates would be arrested and I now had the power of the game's creators at my back.

Not yet. Not until I have fulfilled my obligations and complete Apollo's Lockout.

I couldn't help but smile at the idea that even after I had given in to Wona, I still had to do a dungeon. That being said, my curiosity of what Heaven had in store made me giddy when I realized that I would be one of the first players to set foot there.

I strode toward Heaven's Gates and noticed Sentry Peter looking at me from his podium as I approached.

"Name?" he asked, although his expression showed he recognized me.

"Noah Newbolt."

He flicked through his massive ledger before stopping at a page and running his finger down it. He stopped and nodded.

"It seems all of your sins have been forgiven," he said.

I nodded. "So . . . ?"

Sentry Peter gestured to the gates. "So you may enter."

With a slight creak, Heaven's Gates swung open.

Chapter 26
City in the Clouds

I had been impressed with Dream State settings before, but this was simply awe-inspiring. The first thing it made me think of was a romanticized pre-nuclear American city, but much more colorful, and of course, floating in the sky. Entire blocks of land were lifted up on metallic bases held up by giant blimp-like balloons. They drifted up and down, held together by reinforced bridges that were as solid and as tall as the buildings they led to.

I was like a kid in Disneyland, running up to the first bridge's railing to look down over the side, seeing nothing but clouds and small glimpses of the sea below. As I looked up, a small blimp flew overhead, a poster on its side saying: "Welcome to Heaven. Go by the grace of the Creator."

The first NPCs I passed were enough to confirm my suspicions about the era. Like the NPCs in Land's End, there were men in vests and top hats, as though dressed for some formal occasion. The women were dressed similarly but nothing as over-the-top as the peacock plums in New Calandor. The wealthier-looking NPCs wore goggles, which made sense, considering how close they were to the sun. The bright light shone down on the bouncy blonde hair and blue eyes of the children playing in the street.

At the end of a bridge was an intersection of land which had a large statue of a man holding a rifle. Although the flowing clothes and facial hair were hiding it, I could've sworn I noticed a resemblance between the statue and Windsor Wona himself.

He's put a lot of himself into this one. Maybe too much.

As few of them as there were, it was odd to see vintage motor vehicles pass me by on roads so high up in the air. One that resembled an antique wagon nearly fell on its side when turning a corner. It stopped at the edge of a brick road that led out into nowhere, coughed a few times as it waited for a bridge to connect, and then took off down another row of colorful houses.

A game designer's passion project, perhaps? I guess it fits this era better than the others in this world.

The shopping district seemed to be a long line of these interconnecting islands, each one with a different store to cater to whatever was needed in the Dream State. With unlimited Moola, I was excited to begin shopping, but I wanted to look around a bit more to see what I'd sold my soul to the corporate devil for.

I continued over the bridges that connected the many structures holding up the city like a floating spider web. The buildings loomed over me, colorful flowers hanging from the high balconies and large banners that blew in the wind over the road. Being above most of the clouds, everything was bathed in warm sunlight, showing how beautiful the city really was.

I passed the many NPCs, hearing the jovial, scripted dialogue between them. Whenever someone stared at me or remained silent when I passed, I could assume they were either administrators or Hero rank players confused at seeing a new face in such an exclusive area. I could usually tell this by what they were wearing, but after seeing the fashion in New Calandor and Land's End, I wasn't always sure.

Like most cities and towns in the Dream State, Heaven was a non-combat zone, but knowing this didn't make me feel any calmer. Having been on the run from Wona for so long, I was used to being on my toes just in case things turned sour. I felt justified in this fear—after all, I recalled how Catastrophe had stormed New Calandor when searching for me, showing that the 'non-combat rule' didn't apply to everyone.

Eventually I found the Synth Square. It was near the back of the floating city, and like with every other setting in the Dream State, the way the shops were set up wasn't just unique, but done in a way that it couldn't really be considered a square anymore. All of the stores were on the equivalent of a shopping Ferris wheel. When the right store spun up to the bridge, a player would cross over, and have to the wait for the bridge to appear again before getting off.

A revolving shopping arcade. I see what they're going for, but still, it's a bit much.

Now that I had infinite Moola, I thought I'd make the most of it and buy as many spells as I could. I had everything unlocked now after all. The spell shop slowed to a stop in front of the bridge and I stepped onto the floor. It shook a little as it started to ascend and bring me along with it in its rotation.

Inside wasn't a light fountain like in the Galrinth spell shop, but an open back wall with a full view of Apollo's Lookout. It clearly showed the sun that rose far above the lighthouse.

It wasn't until I saw the dozen streams of light shooting off from it that I realized something about the Dream State that had remained a mystery to me since I had entered. Why were certain areas in constant daylight when others were always set at night? Yet I had noticed that whenever there was light in an area, the sun was always coming from the north.

Does that mean . . . Apollo's Lookout was created under the sun of this world? Considering there are no day-night cycles in the Dream State, a stationary sun makes sense.

I had no way to confirm it, but it felt like I was on to something. Nevertheless, I approached the counter and a list of spells appeared. My mouth dropped when seeing that there were not just level one spells, but level two spells up for sale also. I could buy every spell I hadn't unlocked yet, including the second level of those spells as well.

That means I can get all of the protective magic Keri has!

I gawked and went about splurging with my endless funds. Some say shopping can be therapeutic. This goes double for someone who has been frugal their entire life. Light shot into me from the sun with each one I bought. Regeneration, Protection, Toxin, Rush, and the second level of Enrage; Madness, I bought them all. I didn't even know what half of the spells I purchased did.

A sudden urge to buy more came over me, and in a mad dash, I strode back out of the shop as soon as it met the bridge, turned, and waited for the weavers' store. Inside was a man with a mustache at a desk and behind him seemed to be yet another revolving wheel with every garment I had seen in the Dream State, and many more I hadn't.

I scanned over the gear I could get. Using the Red Goo I collected from the Sulphur Pit, I could make myself a long garment with twice as much magic and attack defense as my Night Down Robes. It was called a 'Captain's Coat' and it was the exact same coat that had been worn by the boss in Pirate Cove.

I didn't hesitate to buy it. The scarlet material was fitting considering the red logo of the company I was agreeing to work with. With a flash, the coat appeared around me. It was fine and looked more like a long duster with a mantle and hood than the wizard's robes I had been wearing.

Deciding to go all out, I bought some leather pants, boots and gloves to go with it. I stepped back onto the platform, feeling proud of my new wardrobe but was far from done with my shopping spree.

Nearly twenty minutes later, I made my way back to the market with more of a swagger in my step than when I'd entered. Having glimpsed another gunstaff that I thought might suit my new gear, I made my way back to the market bridges to see if I could track it down. With all of the abilities and garments I could want now in my possession, I figured picking out a new weapon should be my next priority.

I found the bridge I had been looking for and stepped into the forge. The place had two rooms, a reception and a display area for its armory. When I recognized a familiar face, I froze. The look Data gave me when he saw me in my new clothing was enough to make my skin crawl. The shock and confusion on his face turned to rage as he grabbed me by my coat and pulled me outside.

He practically carried me behind the building before gripping my collar and pushing me against the brick wall. With the place facing the sun, a shadow loomed over us, making Data's glare even more intimidating.

"The heck are you doing here?" he growled, as though hoping the obvious answer wasn't the correct one. "Don't tell me . . ."

I decided not to screw around with him. "I've made a deal with Wona."

"Tsh, you idiot!" He pulled and then pushed me back into the wall. "You have no idea what you've gotten yourself into!"

"I do! Trust me Data, I know exactly what I'm doing." I sighed. "The contract isn't even confirmed yet, not until I meet their obligations. I'm on my way to do that now, so . . . if you don't mind."

I went to brush him aside, but he gripped my coat again and brought me back to face him. "What dungeon?"

When I wouldn't tell him, he shouted the question, his eyes insistent. "I know one of your obligations is to complete a new dungeon! Every player contract has one. What dungeon is it?"

"Apollo's Lookout!" I burst out, pointing to the shining

lighthouse in the distance.

Data let me go and I went to move on.

"I wouldn't have wished what you're doing on anyone. I can't imagine what Wona told you to make you do such a one-eighty, but whatever it is . . ." He shook his head. "It's not worth it, Noah. If you fulfill their obligations, they'll own you."

I grinned back at him. "That didn't stop you from helping us."

"Tsh, you have no idea what I risked by doing that!" He shook his head. "Just think about it before you go through with it."

I turned to leave, jaw clenching involuntarily at his words.

I have already thought about it. If I'm the leader of Catastrophe, the most powerful party under them, what have I got to fear?

Deciding not to waste any time, I turned and made my way toward the lighthouse. As far as this dungeon went, my Boomstick would have to do.

Chapter 27
Apollo's Lookout

So, this is my final stage to becoming Wona's puppet.

The lighthouse that was built under the very sun of the Dream State could be seen from miles away. However, it wasn't until I was directly in front of it that I realized how massive it actually was. It seemed to need a balloon island all to itself, as Apollo's Lookout was as wide around as most city blocks.

The large doors were closed to the outside world and I was shocked something of this size could float this high up in the air, even in a virtual world. As my vision wandered over the beautiful garden that encircled it, I noticed someone was waiting for me outside the lighthouse, leaning against it with his arms crossed. From his red hair, I knew it could only be one person.

Dice smirked at me as I approached. "Hello there."

My brow furrowed. "What are you doing here?"

"The boss thinks it's best you know from the get-go that I hated Bitcon as well. I was also hired by Wona *after* your accident, so obviously I had nothing to do with it. As for the rest, my only excuse is that I was following orders, which should show you how loyal I am to the company."

"So Windsor asked you to tell me this?"

Dice bowed his head and raised his hand, as though pinching the brim of a hat that wasn't there. "He thinks it would be a waste of my training if you were to fire me outright without giving me a chance to prove my loyalty to you. He . . . asked me to accompany you on this dungeon so we can . . . get to know each other a little better."

I nodded and gestured to the large double doors. "Have you done this dungeon before?"

Dice shook his head and straightened. "As far as I know, it's a Tertiatier dungeon that isn't yet completed. It has six floors, each with a high ceiling and its own Chaos Engine. The goal is to reach the roof, but as someone who hasn't tried it before, I can't say how difficult that is. Also, because of its link with the city, this dungeon doesn't allow players to use mounts, so you can't just fly to the roof."

I remembered the sign on the Heaven's Gates platform saying: *"NO STEEDS HEREAFTER"* and wondered if this was the case for the whole city.

"I'm honestly surprised you were given permission to try it out this early in its creation." Dice looked up its length with a protruding bottom lip. "In other words . . . you should be ready for anything."

"I see . . ." I said and moved forward. "Well, let's get this over with."

Before I change my mind.

When I came within a meter of the huge double doors, they opened with a boom that echoed throughout the bottom level. I looked into the large, open hall of shadows on the ground floor. As I stepped inside, my footsteps sounded hollow on the incredibly dusty floorboards.

I noticed in the gloom a rotting staircase that spiraled up and around the brick and mortar walls toward the second floor. The stairs began at the back of the hall and in the space between us and them was what looked like a billowing black cloud. It was the first Chaos Engine of the dungeon.

When the cloud shrank and converged into a single form, it wasn't in the shape of a monster, but a man. Without his helmet I almost didn't recognize him, but when I did, I halted. Despite being a character in the game, when his eyes opened, the Dark Warrior seemed to recognize me as well.

Just as when Data, Siena and I had fought him, the Dark Warrior had long, fair hair that flowed out over his black shoulder armor. He wore a mantle of skulls and a long red cape that fell in waves down his back. Of all of the enemies I had beaten in my time in the Dream State, he was the one that seemed to have had the most thought put into him, but his story had not yet been completed.

But why is he here?

"You were the first to defeat me." The man's blank eyes lifted to the light behind us. "I have fought many battles since, losing some, but winning many more."

I nodded, figuring this to be the case after how desperately Siena, Data and I had fought to defeat him. "Data said you were a knight fallen from grace, but I never did find out why you went mad and forced the druids into the Cursed Pool to make them lose themselves to their magic."

The Dark Warrior's eyes drifted down. "I never went mad. I discovered that the druids were potting against my father . . . the king of the Ice Castle in Lucineer. So, I pretended to want to join the order of the druids myself, my own father disowning me when hearing of this, but it needed to be done!

"I invited all of the druids to the Cursed Pool for my initiation ritual. There, my fellow soldiers awaited them. When they had all arrived, my men emerged from the darkness and pushed each of them into the pool. The waters drove them mad. Guilt stricken with what I had done, I remained at the top of the Keep, the king of my own castle."

Dice's eyebrows knitted in confusion. "You talk to this NPC as though he's a player."

I grinned. "Like Sentry Peter, his A.I. is a little superior to your average gawker in the street." I turned back to the Dark Warrior. "So why are you here? Did a Chaos Engine just happen to bring you?"

He looked troubled. "I'm not certain, but something is telling me to guard this place . . ." He raised his massive sword. "And stop you from going any further."

I nodded. "So be it . . . Dice!"

"Gotcha!" he called and the Ruby Edge flashed into his hand.

He ran in and engaged in a melee against the Dark Warrior, and, although he was a Range Niche, he was holding his ground nicely, not overreaching in fear of getting cut. It was for good reason. I had seen how much damage a single cut by the knight could do.

I moved around the two, launching spells from my Boomstick. The last time I had fought the Dark Warrior, my level one spells had barely dented his Hit Points. Now using Graviton to slow him down, and Wildfire to burn him, Dice and I were taking large chunks off of his Hit Points with relative ease.

Dice was struck once by the long blade and seemed surprised when I used my Regeneration spell to restore his Hit Points.

"Thanks!" he called.

Knowing I was there to back him up, he began fighting with more confidence. He engaged and struck with the Ruby Edge as the Dark Warrior forced down on him with the weight of his armor. The Dark Warrior pushed him off and struck quickly, using the same speed I had remembered him using against Siena.

However, Dice was swifter and managed to get in two fierce blows before jumping back to allow me a turn to cast my spells. I used an Ice Coffin to freeze him and then exploded the icicle around him with a Plasma Beam, the impact of the two attacks sending his Hit Points down to the last tenth.

He was moving sluggishly as Dice cut him down, taking out his remaining health.

The fact that the fight was such a cake-walk with just the two of us showed the obvious improvement to my equipment and skills. As the Dark Warrior fell to his knees before us, I realized the importance of this battle.

I see, there is no real fall from grace when one chooses to do the right thing for others. Like me, the Dark Warrior was only doing what was right to protect those he cared for.

However, there was something in his smile just before he vanished that made me second-guess this idea. The smile showed an underlying look of sadness and pity for me, as though understanding the hard road I would have to take.

"Of all places, why here?" he asked.

Then, just like at the top of the Druids' Keep, he vanished into the air.

Until next we meet.

"What an odd monster," Dice murmured, face screwed up in bafflement.

I shook my head. "He was not a monster. He was a true hero." I strode swiftly to the back of the lighthouse toward the stairs. "Come on, we don't know what might be on the next floor and I want to get this done before the end of the day."

Dice nodded and chased after me as we ascended the stairs. They were steep and we only had to do one lap around the massive wall before we were moving through the rectangular hole that led to the second floor. As soon as I saw the face of the Heavy in his newly synthed Diamond Armor, I realized that the random encounters of the Chaos Engines weren't going to be so random after all.

Chapter 28
Another Lucky Find

As soon as Frank was allowed access to New Calandor, she was curious about why it was called *New* Calandor. That was until she was invited to do a dungeon with Siena's team called the Calandor Ruins. Originally Calandor must have once looked like it had been a twelfth century fortress in the hills, as there were large cannons between the crenulations.

Now the castle was just broken stone that a waterfall ran through, most of the rock from the city walls was at the bottom of the gorge, sticking out from the pool below. Yet as Siena, Chloe, and the rest went ahead of her, the cannons continued to draw her attention.

I'm a tank, I wonder if I could use one of these?

After she had gotten her full set of Dragon Armor, which protected her fully from fire magic, Frank had realized she could carry more equipment than a regular tank could because of her low weight stat.

Gazing at the cannon, she noticed it was actually an item with its own stats that she could take. She shrugged and made it vanish into her inventory, thinking that it might come in handy later on.

— ACQUIRED 'ARCHAIC CANNON' —

She ran to catch up with the others, not used to her armor making her so sluggish, but happy that she could return to people simply assuming she was a guy.

This identity thing is getting too complicated. Maybe I should just alter my avatar to be a male Heavy to prevent confusion.

"Enjoying that Dragon Armor I helped you get?" Siena asked.

I would enjoy it more if you wouldn't keep reminding me you helped me to get it.

"Yeah . . . thanks for that?" She looked around in confusion. "This has very few monsters in it for a Tertiatier dungeon."

Chloe dropped back with her usual frown. "It seems that another party has been in this dungeon recently. The monsters haven't had a chance to respawn yet."

Siena grinned. "Don't worry, though. Most of the stronger monsters here are fire type. With the armor I helped you to get, they shouldn't be too much trouble for you."

"Alright . . ."

I'm beginning to think she'll never let me live this down.

David turned and walked back along the ruined floor, looking over the huge drop to the pools below. "Even so, we're coming to the end and we haven't seen a single monster.

It's like there aren't any here."

Frank noticed he was wearing his immaculate new Diamond Armor that he had synthed from the Resource Items collected in Diamond Hollow. For armor made up of diamonds, its lack of transparency made her think they were incredibly clouded diamonds.

Perhaps that's a good thing, it wouldn't look as cool if I could see his underwear.

Chloe, who seemed to really like correcting David, spoke up. "Or . . . the guys ahead of us are *really* good, or . . . the boss at the end of this dungeon is just *really* hard."

"I'm not sure which one I would prefer to face," Keri said, sounding nervous about being attacked by either a strong monster or a strong group of players.

Siena grinned and rubbed her hands expectantly. "I know right! I can't wait to find out either!"

She only seemed to be paying attention to Keri's words and not how they were said. Frank was beginning to assume that, for Siena, excitement and fear were synonymous with each other.

They eventually came to a huge outcropping that led out over the crashing waterfall to the swamped ruins below. On the stone outcropping were two leaping figures, a giant monster and a single Warrior. The monster was a massive red frog that was jumping from ledge to ledge along the gorge before lashing a fiery tongue at the mysterious Warrior, but that wasn't what shocked Frank.

Their entire party stopped when they saw what the Warrior was wielding. It was exactly like Siena's Color Blade, however, instead of being ruby-red, it was a light amethyst-purple. Frank couldn't believe her eyes. The struggling

Warrior was attempting to swing it at the frog, but the frog continued to jump out of the way until stopping to launch its fiery tongue at him.

He dodged and spotted them, calling out desperately, "You . . . a little help please!"

Siena didn't hesitate to run in with her scythe to help him. "Come on, Efty! This monster won't stand a chance with the armor I helped you to get."

Frank followed her in. "*Okay*, I get it!"

David ran in as well, and Keri began casting support magic on them while Chloe started firing her revolvers at the frog. Puffs of powder hit the frog and it fell back onto the platform, its blazing tongue lashing at Siena. Siena jumped and it hit the other Warrior instead, lowering his Hit Points to below ten percent.

The frog then spat a shower of fire at Frank and David. Siena was right. Although the goopy saliva burned like napalm, Frank barely felt it and it didn't make a dent on her Hit Points, which surprised her for an attack from a Tertiatier level boss. Frank raised her Broadsword and struck at one of the frog's hind legs.

"Enrage me, you idiot support!" the Warrior demanded of Keri.

Keri sounded sour. "Then stop jumping around!"

It was the first time Frank had heard the shy girl snap like that. However, just as she predicted, the Warrior jumped away and Keri's spell missed. Instead of hitting the Warrior, the Enrage spell hit the frog. Everyone gasped

"Oh no!" Keri cried earnestly. "I'm so sorry!"

"Pull back!" Siena called, knowing how terrible a boss could be in the short time that it was affected by the Enrage spell.

All of them but the Warrior did so. Trapped on the other side of the frog, he continued to strike at it with his purple sword. The boss's leg struck out and hit the Warrior hard. The player flew back into a rock wall and his Hit Points took another drop. Too much of a drop.

With an explosion of particle effects, the Warrior vanished. His Color Blade fell and pierced into the mossy floor of the outcropping where it remained upright. Their eyes drew to it. Everyone stared at it speechlessly for a couple of seconds. If it weren't for Siena, the frog would have killed them then and there. It was continuing to hop about but its speed was dropping visibly.

"None of us will get it if we don't kill this thing!" She raised her scythe. "Come on! The Enrage would have worn off by now, let's go!"

The frog leapt at Frank and her team cut away at it. Chloe continued to fire her guns as Keri continued to heal. Frank managed to get a few hits in, David struck it several times, and, as always, Siena managed to finish the fire-spitting thing off. She turned, spinning her scythe behind her as the Frog erupted into a hail of flames.

She grinned as her weapon vanished from her hand and she stepped between her and David, stopping in front of Chloe and Keri. They all turned to face her, standing between them with a raised brow.

"Now, let's make a vote on who gets the Color Blade. It's the fairest way." She narrowed her eyes at us. "And you can't vote for yourself."

There was silence for a moment. A sudden rumble then came over the entire castle, the outcropping trembling from it. The floor beneath them shook and they looked at each other, baffled. Beside her, a blinding light covered David and he vanished from the castle stones. The four of them grew even more confused, when the same light went around Siena's body and she also vanished from the dungeon.

"What's going on?" Chloe asked. "Where did they—"

She didn't finish her sentence for she was the next to disappear, leaving just Frank and Keri. She frowned in confusion as the rumbling became worse, as though whatever was causing the others to vanish was causing the entire dungeon to shake. Stones rattled down from the ruins, a few bricks falling from the ledge above them.

Frank's eyes widened and both of them ran for the sword. It didn't matter who got to it first, so long as one of them acquired the item they could decide who could keep it later, but one of them had to get it.

From the light that went around Keri's body, Frank knew she would be the next to go. *It's up to me . . .*

Whatever force had summoned Keri was the straw that broke the camel's back. The floor collapsed and Frank fell from the ruined outcropping. She continued to reach for the blade, which was still stuck in the moss that had been a part of the broken ledge and was plummeting at the same speed.

Her fingertips were mere inches away from touching it when she vanished from the cool dungeon and landed atop a hard wooden floor. She bared her teeth and cursed when the Color Blade vanished from her sight.

Hearing a howling wind all around her, she rolled over and opened her eyes to an almost blindingly bright light above her. She sat up, feeling frustrated, flustered, and confused. Standing, she made her way to the railing of the roof she was standing on . . . and gasped. She rubbed her face in disbelief but then frowned in bafflement, seeing that she was now standing on top of an entirely new world.

Chapter 29

Switzerland

Noah? Wow, new digs? You look good in red." David's eyes narrowed but then sprang open again. "Oh no! There was a Color Blade, like, right there!" He pointed across the hall, but then looked around the second floor of the lighthouse in confusion. "Wait . . . where the heck am I? And who the heck is that? I think I recognize him."

My brow furrowed in suspicion, and when my vision scanned over him, my suspicions were confirmed. For the first time since I had been in the Dream State, a player avatar was given the red-bordered status of a monster when I brought up his visible stats. And of course, this monster had to be one of my best friends.

I get it now. Wona wants me to kill my friends here.

I figured the point of this was to make me break in-game ties with everyone before I entered the company. It was a pretty malicious idea, I admit, but Wona didn't know my friends very well. David in particular could be spoken to in such a way that I could use his ego against him. I knew exactly how to get around this.

"Hey . . . " I said, trying to sound as casual as possible and then pointed to Dice. "This is . . ."

"Daisuke," Dice said with a wave. He was so convincing when he said this that I honestly thought it might be his real name.

"Aw Noah, you made a Japanese friend," David teased.

I nodded. "Listen . . . um . . . this is a new dungeon that I need to get through. In order to do that . . . I have to defeat every monster in it, and a Chaos Engine seems to have confused you with a monster."

David's face pulled back as though he smelled something repulsive. "Wow, that's pretty messed up. I mean, what are the odds it would pick me?"

My thoughts exactly.

I shrugged, pretending to be nonchalant, as though it couldn't be helped. "I know, right? But I *really* need to get through this dungeon."

He stuck out his bottom lip. "Why is getting through this dungeon so important, though?"

I realized I had screwed up as soon as he asked that. My purposeful vagueness about what I had to do had triggered what little skepticism he had. I decided to tell the truth, but in a way that would help him understand.

"President Wona said that if I can do this dungeon, they will drop any charges they have against Brock. I don't know if they're being honest, but I thought doing just one dungeon wouldn't hurt." I bobbed my head from side to side. "But as you can imagine, Brock is against doing any dealing with Wona, so I'm trying to keep it on the downlow."

David frowned in thought. "Brock mentioned something

like that. He messaged me saying that you were going to give Wona the evidence he had stolen. After everything we went through to get it, it didn't really make sense to me why you would want to do that."

Crap, Brock did tell everyone! Oh well, I can still use this.

"Right . . ." I nodded. "Oh yeah, I managed to replicate the videos so there's more than one copy. Giving them a copy was part of the deal."

"How does that help them if the evidence against them is still out there, though?" he asked, still unsure.

I shrugged. "Beats me. All I know is that I have to get to the top of the lighthouse and take out any monsters I find. You wouldn't mind taking a fall for me just this once, would you?"

David smirked. "I'm not that much of an idiot, Noah. If this is a new dungeon, I've got to check it out first!"

I had first thought to recruit him, but knew that he wouldn't want to knowingly get in the way of Brock's goals. He was too loyal for that. However, if I managed to convince him that he was doing Brock a favor by taking a fall, he would do it. I could call David many things, overly emotional, quick to overreact, trusting to a fault, but disloyal wasn't one of them.

"There's a problem about that. Monsters can't leave their designated floor, and since the Chaos Engine labeled you as one, I don't think you can go very far," I lied. "Come on, man. Do this for Brock. Aren't you sick of him never being around because he's being chased from place to place all the time?"

David laughed. "The way he keeps on breaking the law, though, I'm beginning to think he likes it."

I forced a laugh as well. "But you wouldn't want to see him in jail if he got caught, would you?"

His expression became concerned. "Well . . . no."

I gestured a hand out to him. "So by taking a fall in this dungeon, he'd have his charges dropped. Even if he gets caught, they can't prosecute him."

"You serious?"

I nodded, feeling I was finally convincing him. "I hope so. It's still Wona after all, but they've signed a contract and everything. Even if they decide to go back on their promise, we would still have the paperwork to hold against them in Brock's defense if he does get caught."

David was nodding, as though thinking I was making a good point, but still seemed to be weighing it up with the possibility of exploring a new dungeon.

He sighed. "You know I'm not good with all this business crap. If there's a chance it can get Brock out of hot water, I'll let you kill me. Just don't get me dragged into this fight between you two. I'm Switzerland, I want nothing to do with it, you hear me?"

"Okay great, just unequip your Diamond Armor," I said, trying to sound amused, but I was actually a little worried about it. "I couldn't blast my way through that thing even if I wanted to."

Brock spread his hands, as though just remembering I hadn't seen it before. "I know, right? I got it from Diamond Hollow, it's pretty badass."

"It sure is." I waved him on to hurry him up. "Come on, take it off and I'll make this quick. I have a set of moves that will waste you in a matter of a seconds."

"Stop bragging," David whined. "We already know how

much you've improved since you started."

He made his shining armor vanish into his inventory. As soon as it was gone, I pointed my Boomstick at him and froze him into a block of ice with my Ice Coffin spell. Not wasting a second to let him feel the cold, I shattered it with a Plasma Beam. As far as magic went, that combination of level two attacks was more effective on individual opponents than my Wildfire spell, and that was a level three ability.

David broke into shards of ice, dust from the floor flying up from the explosion. I lowered my gunstaff in the silence of the hall after he was gone. I felt cold from doing it, but it had to be done.

Dice sniggered and moved forward to where David's armor and mace had dropped. "Your friend's an idiot, but at least he had some good items."

"Don't touch them!" I shouted, and he stopped, raising his hands innocently.

I moved in and picked them up, storing them in my inventory. "I plan on returning these to him when we see each other next."

"Fine with me," Dice returned and started forward. "Not like I have any use for Heavy gear."

I followed him as we made our way to the spiraling stairs at the back of the lighthouse. "David's loyal to his friends, unlike you who's loyal to whoever's paying you, considering how quick you were to ditch Bitcon."

He shrugged, as though not finding this offensive. "Bitcon was never my friend, I can admit that." He then caught my eye. "Still, I never *killed* Bitcon."

Guilt ran through me at his words, but I held it down. This was only the second floor, and I had to wall myself off from these emotions if I was to complete the dungeon successfully. I was just glad David could be talked into dying without the confrontation turning into a fight. There were other teammates that, if I ran into them, wouldn't be so easy to convince.

Like Siena . . . or Brock.

Because of how wide Apollo's Lookout was, it took a good ten minutes of walking up the stairs before we made it to the third floor. It seemed my thoughts had jinxed me, for what I dreaded turned into reality. As soon as we entered from under the opening in the ceiling, I saw the red headed Warrior standing in the middle of the dusty floor.

Chapter 30

Reclamation

Siena wasn't happy to see me, but she was even less happy to see me with Dice. Her eyes went vacant for a moment, and I suddenly realized she was using the item tracking software she had gotten from Data. When she was finished, she looked up again, and her glare had become a joyful sneer.

"That bastard still has my Ruby Edge," she said, as though announcing him. "I've finally caught you."

Like David, her visible stats showed that she too was counted as a monster in this dungeon. My suspicions had been correct. Having one friend show up due to a dungeon's Chaos Engine was very unlikely, but possible. Two was another story. However, unlike David, I knew I couldn't talk my way out of this one. Still, I tried.

"Siena, I—"

She cut me off. "I'll get to *you* next. At the moment, this bastard has my attention. This is a Tertiatier dungeon, is it not?"

I nodded.

She bared her teeth in a grin. "Perfect."

A long Reaper's Scythe flashed into her hand as Dice stepped out into the middle of the floor, Ruby Edge flashing into his own. Granted, Siena was one of the best players in the game, but fighting against a Wanted *and* Hero rank with a Color Blade was going to be no easy task. I could only watch in anticipation as they circled each other.

"You're a Range Niche," she taunted. "How long do you think you can last in close combat with a Warrior?"

Dice smiled and scratched his chin. "It depends on how much you know about the Shockwave ability."

"It's a wind magic ability that crosses over to the Warrior and Range Niches and allows strikes to extend in a sonic boom from the arc of a slash." She shrugged and caught my eyes. "It's an ability for cowards."

Dice nodded. "Then you should also know that the stronger the weapon, the more powerful the Shockwave is, right?"

Siena inclined her head in a challenge. "So . . . ?"

Dice didn't hesitate. His Ruby Edge began to glow and he swung it down in Siena's direction. A red wave of energy shot from the Color Blade toward Siena. She leapt out of the way as dust exploded up around where she had been. Dice didn't give her time to recover. He swung again and Siena dive rolled to the side and jumped as a wave of red light shot toward her feet.

Each wave of light shook the floorboards, causing dust to rise up around Siena's side of the room. Soon she was barely visible through the cloud and Dice was swinging waves at her blindly. Although I had seen her move before, I couldn't help but be shocked by Siena's speed. As she ran around the edge of the room, Dice followed her with several more Shockwaves.

The attacks continued to build even more dust around the edge of the hall, giving Siena even more cover to hide in. Instead of going the same way she had been running, as Dice had assumed from the way he continued firing Shockwaves in the direction she had been running, from the gentle swirl of the dust, I could see she had turned to run the other way.

She's trying to catch him off-guard.

I first thought I should warn him, but I couldn't. I was compelled to see what Siena would do. When Dice's back was to Siena, she launched herself out of the dust, spinning her scythe behind her like a flag as the dust swirled around her in her attack. It seemed she intended to slice him right through middle, but Dice spun and brought about his Ruby Edge in a counterstrike.

Their blades clashed high and low, Dice spinning in his attempt to intercept an attack that hooked around his sword and tore open the skin on his upper arm. His Hit Points took a dip, but not as much as Siena's did when Dice's Ruby Edge caught her ankle.

She jumped back and he fired another Shockwave at her. Siena danced around it and charged forward again. Dice struck away her first slash and then backed off, defending himself on the back foot.

For a Range, I was impressed with how he managed to keep up with Siena's speed, but from first-hand experience, I knew Siena's scythe wouldn't last long against a Color Blade.

As long as Dice can stay in the battle, it will only be a matter of time before Siena's scythe breaks.

Dice struck back and the power behind his blow cut the

long blade of her scythe cleanly from the shaft. It severed into the floor at his feet as he began his offensive barrage. She was left wielding only a pole, but she spun it like it had been her intended weapon all along.

Despite Dice swinging his Ruby Edge at her again and again, she spun and struck it away, using some fancy footwork to spin him, luring him toward the place where her scythe blade still stuck into the dusty wood.

She hasn't given up on using it yet.

Her intentions seemed obvious, but in the blind heat of the fight, Dice didn't notice the blade in his determination to hit her. Finally, he landed a devastating blow that drove her to the floor, her Hit Points lowering to the ten percent mark.

She rolled to a stop right next to the severed blade, hiding the length of it underneath her. She turned to see Dice standing over her, his Ruby Edge glowing like it did just before he executed a Shockwave.

"A coward's attack, huh?" he asked. "Well, this coward just killed you."

She tongued the inside of her check. "Oh yeah?"

Twisting, she pulled the scythe-blade from under her and stabbed it into his leg, making him stagger. The Shockwave from his swing hit the dust on the floor next to her, blinding me to whatever happened next.

I heard grunts from Dice through the cloud. All that was visible to me was Dice standing over Siena one moment, and Siena standing over Dice holding the scythe-blade the next, after the dust had faded.

"Support!" Dice called to me, now on his knees.

Whatever she had done with that blade, both players had

less than a tenth of their Hit Points left. As much as Dice was trying to become my teammate, I couldn't help but freeze as Siena raised the blade over him.

"Noah, support!" he cried again.

I furrowed my brow, comprehending what had just happened. "You couldn't even win with a Color Blade. Why would I want you on my team?"

Siena grinned and her wide, bloodthirsty eyes lowered to Dice beneath her. Dice's own eyes darted from me to her. Before he could call out again, Siena sank the long scythe-blade into his chest, relinquishing the last of his Hit Points.

Dice vanished in an explosion and the Ruby Edge fell from his hand, clattering onto the dusty floorboards. Without hesitating, Siena bent down and picked it up, reclaiming what was originally hers.

I'm always underestimating you, Siena.

Despite thinking this, Siena's Hit Points were so low that it would only take a single blow from me to finish her off. The monster status that showed up every time I looked at her reminded me of what I had to do.

She'll never work for Wona. Data has offered her a Hero rank a few times now and she always refused.

"Just do it already," Siena murmured and turned to face me with a sour expression. "Come on, Noah, get it over with."

I didn't know if she knew about what I had to do here, but it really didn't matter in the long run. I raised my open hand to cast a Plasma Beam at her.

"I'll give the Ruby Edge back to you when I see you next."

Siena spat. "Don't bother." She grinned at me

threateningly. "I'll kill you and get it off you myself."

Fair enough.

I cast my spell, the beam of light shot from my hand, and Siena was no more. On the bright side, neither was Dice. I moved forward and picked up her Ruby Edge from the dusty floor before making my way to the stairs at the back of the room.

— ACQUIRED 'RUBY EDGE' —

Chapter 31
FEELINGS

Although I felt bad for killing David and Siena, it still felt amazing to be finally holding one of the Color Blades. I was glad it was the red one as well. As vain as I was to think so, it suited my red Captain's Coat perfectly. I was a scarlet Spellcaster now, a red battlemage of both cloth and weapon, the perfect Catastrophe leader for Wona.

I walked up the staircase, my leather boots making hollow thuds against the dead wood. Coming to the fourth floor, I wondered who would be waiting to face me there. I didn't have to wait long, for as soon as I emerged from the opening in the ceiling, a bullet pinged off the wall right beside my head, making me duck.

"Whoops! I thought you were a monster. Hah, remember going with me to buy these guns, Noah? Brock was right, they really have grown on me," Chloe said, her eyes suddenly widening when seeing what was is my hand. "Is that the Ruby Edge?"

I raised it to show her. "I managed to get it for Siena."

She shook her head. "I thought you had something to do

with us being drawn here when you weren't replying to our messages, but even I wouldn't have guessed you would find the blade before us!"

This wasn't entirely true, but I thought it would be useful to make it seem like that to get through to the next floor. "Well, I need to get to the top."

"And I see you have the whole Red Mage thing going on." She raised her brow at my coat and said in a sarcastic tone, "Real nice."

"Chloe, I get you like to act cold and banter to cover up how you really feel with people, but I don't want to fight you so I'll be blunt." I held the Ruby Edge out in front of me.

Chloe aimed her guns at me from the sudden movement. "Is this a trick?"

"No trick." I dropped my hand. "Just the truth."

Chloe lowered her pistols, her expression suddenly open. "Go on."

"I've been given the opportunity to work for Wona, to be paid to play in the Drea—"

"And so you have to kill off all your friends to do that?" she burst out in anger.

I raised my hand again to calm her and she stopped.

"Let me finish." I waited until she blew the breath out of her puffed cheeks. "To do this I have to complete this dungeon and kill whatever's on each floor. However, it's also within my power to employ people for my future team under them, meaning I can allow others to get paid to play here as well. I don't think Wona will make me kill my own team considering they're encouraging me to recruit players to their ranks." I looked up at the high ceiling as though shouting at God. "Isn't that right?

Chloe's confused face became thoughtful, her gaze shifting to the floor. "What did you have to do to get that opportunity? I mean, they wouldn't have just offered you this now for no reason."

"I have to give them the evidence that was on the Transfer Orb."

Her eyes glared into mine again. "So not to kill us then . . . just to sell us out and forget who was responsible for killing your girlfriend?"

"I can see why it might look that way, but what we've been fighting for all this time has been based on a lie." I had tried thinking of ways to say this so many times that I thought I'd finally found the right way to do it. "The crash that killed Sue was executed by a faction of Wona that went rogue, and Wona has promised to have them prosecuted for it. As for the beta testers who died . . . Brock's old friends . . . each of them signed consent waivers not holding Wona responsible for the drugs they took voluntarily. A bad outcome for some of them didn't change that fact."

Chloe nodded uncertainly. "It sounds like you're trying to convince yourself of these things more than me."

"The president himself showed me this, Chloe." I looked down, remembering Brock's lie. "As well as the video of Brock signing his own waiver."

She bit her lip and her eyes shot around the hall. "I think I'm beginning to see where you're coming from. The company wouldn't do those things if they couldn't cover their rear ends. And Brock . . . I'm a little pissed that every time we put our necks on the line for him it was based on a lie. Would they show me the videos as well if I was on your team?"

I shrugged, but much preferred her shooting questions at me than bullets. "I don't see why not."

"I'm still not sure about this, Noah. I mean they're our friends, and—"

"Listen, David and Siena have already failed to stop me, but they would never have joined Wona anyway, especially not Siena." I said, remembering Data's many offers to her. "But I want you and Keri at my side when I do this. I know how much you love to play here. Heck, with my frail body, being in this world feels more normal to me than reality. Spreading the evidence will not only cause Brock to break his contract with them and make him a criminal, but it might also destroy the very thing that we have all come to love."

Chloe seemed to think for a while.

I've played my best cards. It's all up to her now.

Finally, she sighed and met my eyes. "To be honest, I never wanted the Dream State to get shut down. I was just playing with you because . . ." She looked down as though embarrassed. "And I didn't think we would actually . . ."

"You like me, I get it, and I like you, too. You've stolen two kisses from me already, and it only took me one to realize." I gestured to the floor above us. "And you love this game as much as I do, so come with me and we can play here as much as we want and get paid to do it!"

Come on. I have to get a least one of them on my side.

She stepped closer to me and looked down. "I want to."

I knew I would have to do this. I used my finger to tip her chin up so she was looking into my eyes. Then, for the first time, I kissed her.

Keri and I may have once had some chemistry between us, but that had passed, and after I realized that Sue was really dead, I had no reason to hold back anymore. Chloe's body seemed to tense, but then relax as I pulled her into an embrace.

When she pulled away and whispered, "Okay," I knew I had her.

"Alright, now we just need to convince Keri and we'll be good to go."

Chloe looked back down, as though understanding that this would be an inevitable complication in my plan. "Let me talk to Keri. I know her better than you, I'll be able to convince her more easily."

I smiled down at her, realizing this would make the process a whole lot easier. "Alright . . ." I then shouted as loud as I could so that whoever was watching could hear me. "You hear that? Chloe is going to be on my team, so take away her monster status!"

I knew that if nothing happened I might end up looking like a complete idiot, but thankfully as Chloe passed over my vision again she had returned to having the blue ally status. This made it so if I could convince the others. I wouldn't have to defeat them to complete the dungeon.

This left me with only one question: Who will be the friend on floor number five?

While we ascended the stairs, I made sure that our views were in line. We had to make sure our stories were straight if we were to run into Keri and convince her to team up with us as well. We had several things that we clearly agreed upon.

We both thought that a confirmation that Sue's killers would be arrested was far better than the weak hope that Wona would be held responsible for the death of every beta tester that overdosed. We both thought that Brock was risking too much in breaking his contract to get the information out to the public. Most importantly, we were both clear in our desire to work for Wona and be paid to play the game.

"And I think I can convince Keri of the same!" She walked closer beside me. "She's decided for herself to spend her time in this game, so that's a given. If we can just get her to see that what Brock is doing is hopeless, we might be able to . . ." She trailed off and looked down.

"What's wrong?"

"Keri has always been a helpless romantic. If she finds out about us . . ."

I frowned and nodded in agreement. "Best not to bring that up yet. No need to make things more complicated than they already are."

Chapter 32
The Moral Good

With the situation as complicated as it was, I wanted to make a good first impression with Keri. Despite this, she seemed startled by our sudden appearance when we arrived on the dusty floorboards. Panting after climbing the massive stairwell and running out onto the fifth floor, she turned to us with a frightened jump.

"Chloe!" she called, as though happy to see a familiar face. "When you and the others vanished, everything was shaking! I couldn't get the Color Blade before a light surrounded me and I showed up here!"

"It's okay, Keri. Everything's fine," Chloe said as she rushed over to calm her.

Keri looked at me in puzzlement. "N-Noah, why are you here? You weren't with us in the Calandor Ruins."

Chloe stepped forward. "I found him here. Listen Keri, there's something we have to tell you."

Keri's brow furrowed, her voice concerned. "What is it?"

"Brock's been lying to us. Turns out even if we did get the evidence of the videos out to the public, it wouldn't do anything to Wona because the beta testers signed a consent waiver so that Wona wouldn't be responsible for whatever happened to them."

Maybe it was because I had been Brock's friend for a while, or maybe it was because Chloe had more practice at being like this, but I hadn't even thought of explaining myself by attacking his position first.

Keri covered her mouth with her hands. "But the videos . . . they would allow people to know what Wona did, wouldn't they?"

"That's true," Chloe said, sounding consoling. "But if we did that, Brock would have broken the law. He signed a confidentiality agreement, and by showing people the videos, he would have shared private information."

Keri shook her head. "But he told us it didn't matter, that he was fine being on the run as long as the information was out there." Keri looked from me to her. "But you two already knew all this so . . . why are you saying this now?"

Her expression slowly changed as she took in my long red coat and Siena's Ruby Edge. What Chloe was saying then seemed to dawn on her.

"Are you planning on giving them the videos like Brock said?"

Chloe looked to me in a sudden panic and I pinched the bridge of my nose, realizing that I would have to tell her what we were getting out of it.

"Wona's promised to put the ones who killed Sue in jail if I work for them."

Keri took a step back from us, looking like she had just seen a ghost. "Have you given them the videos yet?"

I shook my head. "They want me to get to the top of this

dungeon first."

Keri ran forward and grabbed my wrist. "Don't do it, please! After what Brock's sacrificed, wouldn't it be better to wait and see how the public will react to them so we can hold the company accountable for what they did to his friends?"

Oh no! David must have told her everything during their time in Diamond Hollow.

"Why are you saying this?" Chloe asked, her voice rising in pitch. "You love the game! Why would you want to do something that could possibly shut it down?"

"I do . . . but even so . . ." Keri looked down, her lip trembling. "I think they should confess to what they did. Even if they did find a way to get away with it, everyone should still know that people's lives were sacrificed to make the game we love! Otherwise, what does it even mean?"

"Keri!" Chloe pleaded. "We have a chance to play this game and get paid to do it! You can be included in on the deal! Don't you want that?"

Keri shook her head. "What's the difference between that and being paid to keep quiet? I'm sorry, you guys, but even if Noah's girlfriend is avenged by having her killers brought to justice, the people that were coerced into signing those waivers won't get their justice if we don't show everyone those videos!"

"Alright, that's enough!" I raised my palms. "I can't complete this dungeon unless I defeat everyone on each floor of this dungeon, okay?"

"So you'll have to kill me?" she asked, her voice high with emotion. "Just so you can give in to Wona?"

I shook my head. "Either that, or you join us. They're the only two options that are available to us at the moment."

Keri sniffed, as though she would be crying in real life, and raised her hand. Her white Spellcaster staff appeared in her grip, ready to defend herself.

"Alright, I'll fight you two, if that's what you want!" she exclaimed but without looking at all happy about it.

Chloe shook her head. "Why are you being so stubborn? It's either confirmed arrests for a murder, or an incredibly unlikely arrest for many. The odds are completely against us!"

"Even so . . ." Keri bit her lip with an expression that if it wasn't anger then it was its nearest cousin. "The latter is the greatest moral good! And if we're not going to at least try to do what's morally good, what are we but evil?"

"Reasonable compromise is evil now?" I asked, my hackles rising from this absolutist mumbo jumbo. It reminded me of one of Sue's bad arguments. "Damn, but did I bet on the wrong horse when we first met."

"That's enough, Noah!" Chloe put her hand out, as though to prevent me from saying anything more that would hurt Keri. "I'll deal with her on my own."

I eyed Chloe's new gunslinger guise, her face expressing her annoyance. "You know what it will mean if you can't—"

"I know, I know, get going!" She waved me toward the staircase at the back of the hall. "I'll either convince her to come with us, or I'll kill her before I leave. Either way, no enemies will be left, alright?"

I shifted my gaze from the fearful expression on Keri's face to the determined expression on Chloe's and nodded. I knew which one I would put my money on. Chloe was a feisty Range fighter who had saved my butt on more than one occasion, while Keri was only a supporting Spellcaster.

However, as I began my climb to the sixth floor, I couldn't help but watch their fight with interest. Keri began by raising a shield spell as Chloe shot at her with her revolvers. The shield was being chipped away at while Keri reinforced her protective defense and spun her wrist like pouring a bottle to cast the Toxin spell.

Oh crap! When did she learn the level two poison spell?

I recalled having that spell used on me by Bitcon's Spellcaster when he was asking me to hand over the Transfer Orb. I knew how effective it could be.

Chloe used an item to increase her speed and began fanning one of her pistols at Keri. Both of their health bars began to descend below the two thirds mark. Keri was casting another spell that looked like time magic to slow Chloe down just as I passed under the ceiling of the fifth floor and emerged onto the sixth.

Finally, I've reach the top floor. Which means my last fight will be with . . .

Waiting for me there was someone I'd once thought of as my best friend. Now he was the one thing stopping me from completing the dungeon. Brock stood there, glaring at me. However, the weapon he was wielding told me more than any words he might have spoken could have.

Grasped in his hand was the Sapphire Edge, Data's blue Color Blade. It seemed to take me joining Wona for Brock and Data to finally forgive each other and work together. Work together to stop me, that is.

Chapter 33
Splitting Waves

We stood there, our red and blue Color Blades glowing in the dim light like two opposing lightsabers. We were going to fight; that was inevitable. Unlike the others, I knew I wouldn't be able to talk my way out of this. Our goals were not just different, but opposing. One of us couldn't succeed without the other failing.

"I see you and Data have made amends," I said.

"He apologized to me for being wrong. He was telling me what was going on before I appeared here. We continued messaging each other and he sent me this as a file." He raised the Sapphire Edge. "I'm to use it to stop you from completing this dungeon."

Data's found a way to try and stop me without even being here. So . . . Brock represents his desires as well. But it's not the first time I've felt betrayed by him.

"Now we both have one." I grinned and raised my Ruby Edge. "It's nice to know good things are already coming from me joining Wona."

"Stop kidding around!" Brock shouted. "I get that a part of the reason why you're doing this is to protect me. Don't bother, I can take care of myself. As for Sue, she would have achieved her goal if these videos are received by the public. Wona will be taken down in the way that she had wanted."

I shook my head. "There's a problem with that, though. If my plan fails, you can still try to take down Wona. But if your plan fails, everything fails."

"What?" Brock's eyes became fierce. "Why?"

"Unlike you, I read their contract before signing it." I ground my teeth. "They have Double Jeopardy Clauses in their contracts! Do you know what that means?"

Brock shook his head, obviously clueless.

"It means that once the entire company is pulled up on charges and gets away with it, which it will because of the consent waivers you and your friends signed, no one in that company can be held up on the same charges. That means no one, not Bitcon, not Colban, no one, will be arrested for what they did to Sue!" I poked a thumb at my chest. "But I'm not going for Wona! I'm just going for those who killed Sue, and Wona is helping me to do that! Until then, all you're doing is guaranteeing that they'll get away with what they did!"

I may have been stretching the truth of what a Double Jeopardy Clause could do, but I could see from Brock's shaking composure that it was definitely having the effect I had been hoping for. It seemed the little research I did into law terminology before signing on with Wona really turned out to be useful.

However, Brock's shocked expression then became a smirk. "Only a couple of hours with Wona and you're already arguing like a businessman."

I was flabbergasted that he didn't register what I was saying. "What do you mean?"

Did he see through my lie or is he just being stubborn?

"You care way too much about the law and contractual agreements. What about when public opinion turns on them?" Brock smiled in his conviction. "If nothing else, that alone will destroy their business!"

"You have too much faith in people."

"And you have too little!" he spat back.

I sighed and said coldly, "I see there's no getting through to you. I only have one thing left to say:" I lined up my Ruby Edge with his head. "Get out of my way."

"No."

Brock charged at me. I stepped in and struck at him in turn. He parried and countered, but I managed to catch it on my Ruby Edge, swinging out with all my strength, knowing from experience that the Color Blades could not break.

Brock leapt back from my swing and rushed in again. Neither of us were Warriors equipped for a melee. That being said, having trained myself as a battlemage, I'd had more practice at swordplay. This was shown as we clashed and I managed to force him backward, slashing at him with quick strikes. Yet I could see from him keeping up with me that the Range Niche obviously had more base speed than Spellcasters.

I cast the second level of Speed Amp, Rush, on myself. This gave me much more of an edge over Brock as I dashed at him, swerving around his downward strikes and spinning into a wide slash. Brock ducked but wasn't quick enough to dodge as I launched a Plasma Beam at him, sending him flying and taking down his Hit Points by a quarter.

With my new spells, I've pretty much won this already.

However, as Brock recovered from my beam, he spun to his feet and raised the Sapphire Edge. It began to glow a bright blue and I gasped when realizing that he knew about the Shockwave ability.

He's a Range fighter just like Dice! Of course he would know about an ability for his own Niche!

He launched the Shockwave and the arc of energy shot toward me. Still sped up by my spell, I managed to dodge it, but with it came two more that I was only just lucky enough to evade. My thoughts rushed in an attempt to think of how I could counter these attacks. Then an epiphany hit me. I had bought every ability possible while in Heaven's Synth Square.

I cast an Ice Wall spell, hoping that it would hold out against his Shockwave onslaught while I brought up my full screen menu and searched my abilities for it. My assumption that it was just an ability for Range and Warriors was proven wrong when I found it among the many abilities I had accumulated.

There was a crash and my ice wall crumbled, ice flying at my back. I quickly used my finger to drag the Shockwave ability into my Key Triggers, then rolled to the side as I noticed another blue arc rushing at me in my peripheral vision. It missed, but only just.

Okay, let's see how this ability holds up against itself!

Brock sent yet another Shockwave my way, but before the horizontal arc could reach me, I selected the ability and swung out. My own arc of red energy shot forth and parted the blue one heading my way. Instead of hitting me, the wave separated and shook the rock walls on either side of me.

Brock cut my own wave in two with one of his own and we continued to trade blows, striking out at each other's waves. The rock walls trembled and dust rose from the floor just like in the fight between Siena and Dice. Being the top floor, there wasn't as much dust to create cover, but it still distracted me from what was occurring in the corner of my vision as we continued to go Shockwave for Shockwave.

It wasn't until the blue Mana bar in the corner of my screen started going red that I realized my mistake. Shockwaves may have been a ranged attack, but like my Ice Regeneration and Instant Reforge ability, it took a small bit of Mana each time it was used. Because I had used three level two spells in the course of the fight, my Mana had already been low before I'd even discovered the Shockwave ability.

I'm going to run out, and then I'll be a sitting duck! I should have used Graviton when I had the chance!

I cast another Ice Wall, hoping Brock using his Shockwaves against it might lower his Mana enough to make us even, but it was to no avail as he simply used one of his Mana regeneration arrows on himself. As I sat there behind the wall, something about seeing the Shockwaves cut through each other triggered a memory of when I had asked Data if the Color Blades needed maintenance.

"No, it's one of the few qualities that makes it so handy."

If they don't break, they should be able to cut through the Shockwaves as well, shouldn't they?

Although I was acting on very little evidence, I figured it was better than just waiting for my Mana to run out. I stood and slowly walked out from behind the scarred wall of ice.

"Finally stopped trying to delay the inevitable, huh? I've always been looking out for you . . . every time you did a Tertiatier dungeon . . ." Brock raised the Sapphire Edge. "But no more." The blue glow roared to life inside the blade before he swung it down in a rippling arc. "No more!"

I bared my teeth, and as soon as the Shockwave was about to hit me, I slashed through it with my blade. The wave parted and went around me, hitting the wall behind me. It had worked. I glared at Brock and started to walk toward him.

"What?" Brock's eyes widened. "No!"

He launched another blue arc of energy my way. Raising the Ruby Edge, I cut through it and continued walking. Brock knew once I got him into close quarters the fight would be over, and he desperately attempted to fire another Shockwave to the same effect. I cut it in half and sped up my advance, casting Madness on myself to increase both my speed and strength.

"Fine!" Brock shouted. "If that's how it is!"

We struck once, twice, engaging into a fierce struggle. I forced him off me and began cutting. He parried with swift movements, going blow for blow, but I knew it was over. I blitzed him with a series of strikes and close range level one magic that left him stunned. Tripping him with a Wind Blast, I proceeded to rain heavy blows down upon him.

On one knee, Brock raised his blade against mine, the only thing shielding him from my onslaught, but it wasn't enough. I struck it aside with one hand, and blasted him with a Plasma Beam with the other, bringing his Hit Point down to a tiny fraction.

I rose and he glared up at me.

"It's funny, when I first started this game, I looked up to you," I said, feeling slightly exhausted from the fight. "Now look at you."

"No . . . you didn't." Brock shook his head, grinning despite his obvious defeat. "As a Spellcaster, even in the beginning you were a little taller than me. With the height difference, you were always looking down on me."

I shook my head, amused that he would bring up something so trivial in such a situation. "Get a life, Brock. After all, you'll be able to after this."

Brock inclined his head. "Not you, though."

I nodded and raised my Ruby Edge. "I've made my decision."

"Oh yeah?" He raised a brow at me "Just as I made mine?"

I stabbed the Color Blade down, taking out the last of his Hit Points. He vanished from the top floor hall, his leathers and the Sapphire Edge dropping onto the dusty wooden boards. Seeing it laying there, a wide smile played onto my lips

Siena was right on two accounts, two Color Blades are better than one, and I really do like dual wielding.

I picked up the sword.

— ACQUIRED 'SAPPHIRE EDGE' —

At first, I wondered why a 'Dungeon Complete' scroll didn't unroll in my vision as well, but then I remembered what Dice had told me. The goal of the dungeon was not to get to the top floor but to reach the rooftop. I located a ladder leading up the wall and made my way over to it.

Looking up, I noticed a hatch in the ceiling.

I began to climb. As one would expect of a coned-shaped structure, the hall at the top floor was narrower than its base. However, that didn't make the ceiling any lower, and it took a long time of climbing to finally reach it.

I pushed up the hatch and it slammed heavily onto the roof. The brightness above almost blinded me, but I managed to pull myself up onto the surface and look around. Now outside, the high winds howled around me. Shuddering in exhaustion, I stood and closed the hatch before finally seeing my goal.

I was high above Heaven, the tallest point in the Dream State. Around the edge of the roof there was a chest high railing, and in its center was an empty plinth. I walked over to it and when I looked at its blackened base, words appeared in my vision:

— "You've done well, Noah. Now put the evidence in this loading bay and the dungeon will be complete."—

I sighed in relief now that I had finally finished my test. I was about to pull my Wakizashi out from my inventory and place it inside when I realized there was one more monster I had yet to kill.

"Noah?" asked a familiar brittle voice.

I turned to see FranktheTank standing behind me.

Chapter 34
Only an Annoyance

Of all the people I could have faced in Apollo's Lookout, Frank was the one I wanted to fight the least. Not because I liked him . . . er, her, but because she was just so pathetic, the least likely to be able to defend against my attacks. She wasn't really an opponent, only an annoyance.

I almost feel sorry for her . . . almost.

What was so odd about the encounter was that I actually recognized her new armor, or at least parts of it. The red shoulders, arm guards and gauntlets were exactly the same as the Dragon Arm I had bought from Toena, the very first item I had bought on my own after arriving in the game.

I advanced on her, the Ruby and Sapphire Edges both flashing into my hands. The way she stepped back in confusion showed she had no idea what was going on, and it seemed like she really didn't want to lose her new armor either. It didn't matter. She was in my way.

"Noah, I don't know what's going on here . . ." she said, hands raised in surrender. "But listen, I have a friend who's being bullied by a group called Catastrophe, and Siena said I should ask you about them. She said you might be able to help her."

I stopped. It quickly made sense why she had gone to the Broken Clock Tower as a new player to sell the orb. Catastrophe must have tricked her by using someone she trusted. However, the fact that she wanted to get help against Catastrophe reminded me suddenly of how lost and scared I'd been when they had been after me.

If Brock hadn't been around to help me, I don't know what would've happened.

I made my Color Blades vanish, pulled out the Wakizashi that the videos were encoded onto and held it out to her.

"You see this?" I asked, hoping to be as direct as possible.

She nodded, looking puzzled.

"Well, as soon I as put this blade on that thing." I pointed to the plinth in the middle of the roof. "I will be the leader of Catastrophe and can make them do whatever I want. That includes making them stop bullying your friend. But to do that, I need you to do one thing for me, okay?"

She nodded again, her voice sounding confused and frightened. "What?"

"Say you're going to work for Wona." I shook the short sword in front of her red helmet. "Just say it, okay?"

Knowing Frank was too afraid and too weak to do anything against me, I turned my back on her and walked to the plinth. I stabbed the curved blade of the Wakizashi into the black base and a loading bar appeared beneath it, slowly filling up. It looked like the video files were being downloaded into the game itself.

Is this how I end the test?

Something hit me, hard, and the impact flipped me over the plinth. The force was enough to make me hit the railing that went around the edge of the roof. I looked down, feeling dazed and was shocked to see another large chunk of my health was gone. Then I saw Frank standing on one knee, holding onto what looked like a cannon from an old pirate ship.

"The heck?" I breathed

Frank stood. Only someone of her size could have lifted such a massive weapon. Smoke rose from the barrel of the cannon.

I've heard of a knife in the back before . . . but a cannonball? I bared my teeth, hot anger building inside me. *I have to be careful. That thing packs a wallop, but it should only be able to fire once.*

"Siena told me you were going to sell out your friends." Although I couldn't see her face through the helmet of the Dragon Armor, her voice was trembling. "Is that why everyone vanished?"

I grinned as she staggered toward me, seeing that the large cannon obviously slowed her down a bit.

My Color Blades appeared once again in my hands. "That was a big mistake!"

I went to charge at her. However, my assumption that the cannon could only be fired once was wrong. There may have been a cooldown time, but Frank didn't have to reload before she fired it again.

"No!"

It blasted me back again, the cannonball knocking me through the rooftop railing. I went sailing back off the edge of the building, but managed to empty my hands of the Color Blades and grab the end of the broken railing, dangling out over the edge of the roof. In my panic, I brought out my blue Summoning Stone.

Let's see how this bastard likes the Storm Horn!

Before I could use it, Frank came to edge of the roof and looked down on me, her cannon proving her to be more than just a simple annoyance.

That weapon must have a glitch in this era! It's way too powerful!

As soon as the smoke stopped rising from it, another cannonball shot toward me. Instead of being hit by it and letting it take the rest of my Hit Points, I let go of the railing and fell, preparing to summon Peragon. However, as I looked down, I realized the option to do so wasn't in my Key Triggers.

I gasped as I realized my mistake and the memory of what Dice had told me about Apollo's Lookout suddenly came back to me:

"Also, because of its link with the city, this dungeon doesn't allow players to use mounts, so you can't just fly to the roof."

"Oh crap!"

I screamed and spun in the air to avoid the projectile, watching as the clouds around the lighthouse flew up at me. I tried to do the rolling-hands movement for a Cyclone spell to slow my fall, but even if I had managed to finish the gesture, the thought to cast it had arrived too late.

They say the higher you get, the farther you have to fall. I wish that had been the case. I wouldn't have minded summoning Peragon once I had fallen past the clouds and flown to safety. However, I hadn't been propelled far enough from the lighthouse when I let go of the railing.

The second to last thing I remembered seeing in the Dream Engine was the green of the gardens that encircled the lookout rushing up to meet me. The last was the neon lettering on the inside of my helmet saying:

— GAME OVER —

After seeing Noah fall, Frank rushed over to the plinth. The upload bar was at a hundred percent. She was too late. However, another loading bar replaced it with the word 'Deleting' underneath. She pulled it free before it could start, and as soon as she did, a scroll unrolled in her vision.

— DUNGEON COMPLETE —

So I completed this dungeon by pulling a blade free?

Frank turned to where Noah had emerged from the roof and pulled up the trapdoor to see a ladder leading down. Knowing of no other way of leaving, she used it to climb to the floor below. Finding it empty, she moved over to the stairs leading down and descended under the floor that then became the ceiling.

Keri was sitting in the middle of the floor below, her legs pulled up to her chest. She was looking down at her feet with an expression of sorrow and frustration. Frank rushed to her and she stood up, as though she had been waiting for her.

"Frank, how did you manage to escape Noah?"

She shrugged with a grin. "I guess he underestimated me."

Keri smiled slightly. "I'm impressed. Did you end up getting the Color Blade in the Calandor Ruins? "

"No . . . this place gives me the creeps. I want to leave here ASAP."

"I see . . ." Her eyes widened. "Did you see where the Color Blade landed in the dungeon before you faded?"

Frank shook her head. "But I have a hunch. Let's go."

Keri stood and they moved down the many stairs to get outside.

"I assume everyone in the Calandor Ruins was taken here." Frank looked down at Keri's pensive frown. "Who would have thought that just the two of us would be the only ones to get out of here alive, right? How did you manage to survive?"

"I had to fight Chloe." She looked down. "I don't want to talk about it."

I guess this place was a little weird for everyone.

Frank shrugged and they continued their descent.

The place was so massive it took nearly an hour before they made it down to the ground floor. It seemed to take even more time in the silence between her and Keri. She assumed the dungeon was incomplete by the lack monsters or details inside. The place was just empty.

When they exited the lighthouse, Frank shook her head at the size of the massive floating city they were on. Keri didn't seem at all amazed by the sight.

"My DSD is running out. So I'm going to wake up to log out, okay?" Keri said.

"I'll do the same." Frank waved. "I'll see you the next time we do a dungeon together."

Keri nodded and the world went dark.

Francine pulled free of the game's grip on her and removed her Dream Engine helmet from her head, but she wasn't finished with it yet. She took another dose of DSD and put it back on, returning to the Dream State and heading straight to the Calandor Ruins.

Instead of doing the dungeon properly, she avoided most of the monsters, as well as the Fire Toad, and found the way down to the lowest area. It wasn't until she came to the hollow at the base of the hills that she realized how deep the pool there was. The waterfall that went through the castle ruins ended there, and she looked around at the giant pieces of wall and debris that stuck up from the water.

She searched the base for the Amethyst Edge but saw nothing resembling it. She didn't want to go too far into the water because she knew her armor's weight would draw her to the bottom of the pool and drown her. However, as soon as the thought crossed her mind, she remembered going with Tessa to Mermaid Lagoon to get the ability to breathe underwater before their argument.

Turns out that might not have been such a waste of time after all.

She dragged her Aqua Lungs ability into her Key Triggers. Going into the water was weird, but being able to breathe as she went under was even weirder. The Dragon Armor pulled her down, allowing her to walk along its floor.

The hill that made up the bottom continued going down

into a beautiful underwater valley. From the look of the place, a good portion of the dungeon seemed to be hidden underwater, but only those with the ability from Jossi Island could explore it.

But Jossi Island is a new setting. How many people have even been down here?

She continued to descend, her armor weighing her down as she went deeper and deeper. The castle ruins stretched out underwater like the base of a fish bowl. Aquatic creatures swam in and out of the crumpled structures and Frank knew she should be wary of them while on her own.

At first, she couldn't see anything in the darkness at the base of the valley, but then glimpsed a purple glow being emitted in its center. There at the very bottom, she finally found what she had been searching for.

The outcropping that collapsed must have regenerated and the Warrior who lost it probably thought one of us had already taken it for ourselves. But it's right here. It's been here since we were teleported away.

It was sticking out of an algae-covered rock at the base of the valley. She came upon the Color Blade and marveled at the way the purple luminance turned the water around it a similar hue. She was about to grab hold of it when she realized this was how her encounters with Siena and her group of friends began.

It all began with finding a rare item that I was trying so hard not to let anyone know about. Should I repeat that mistake again, knowing that it will only lead to more people coming after me?

Her hand hovered over the sword's pommel as she contemplated this, remembering everything that had happened to her over the last week. Being chased by Catastrophe, Tessa betraying her, becoming friends with Siena and the rest, and defeating Noah on the rooftop at the highest place of the Dream State. Her memories here had become one big adventure.

No more being indecisive! What's the point of playing this game, if I'm not going to really play it?

She grasped the Color Blade by the hilt and pulled it free.

— ACQUIRED 'AMETHYST EDGE' —

Acknowledgements

I'm beginning to think all of these books are going to come out of car crashes.

A few days into writing Back in the Game, I realized I only had enough story for a third of the novel. I was lucky, however, that on the way to dinner that evening I was in a minor car accident. The apathy I had toward the plight of the other driver when I just wanted to go and eat dinner made me feel like a villain. This feeling stayed with me until Hayley suggested I do what I had originally intended for book one and make Brock a villain. I couldn't do that. Brock was just such a good guy . . . but Noah was another story, and along with what I'd felt after the crash, ideas began to take root.

From that point on, the book pretty much wrote itself. All up, it took about two weeks to complete the first draft, but it was a mess. Jack Gifford, my invaluable first reader, edited it into a state of legibility, a task I would argue was even more difficult than the writing itself. He did this in even less time than it took to write the book, hence the dedication. Hayley picked up where Jack left off, finally being able to enjoy the fruits of our discussion weeks earlier. I sent it away and my editor, Mandi Diaz, caught many of the plot holes that we had missed and that was that. All of these people, even the driver who crashed into us, deserve acknowledgements.

I also have to thank Jeff Harvey for the cover art and everyone at Future House Publishing for the hard work they put into this book and getting it out there. Thanks also to my readers, I hope to bring you a third volume in the future.

About the Author

Growing up in the small town of Timaru, New Zealand, Christopher Keene broke the family trend of becoming an accountant by becoming a writer instead. While studying for his Bachelor of Arts in English Literature from the University of Canterbury, he took the school's creative writing course in the hopes of someday seeing his own book on the shelf in his favorite bookstores.

He is now the published author of the Dream State Saga, as well as his new epic fantasy trilogy, A Cycle of Blades. In his spare time, he writes a blog to share his love of the fantasy and science fiction genres in novels, films, comics, games, and anime (fantasyandanime.wordpress.com).

CPSIA information can be obtained
at www.ICGtesting.com
Printed in the USA
FSHW010643061219
64684FS

9 781944 452810